Persona Non Grata

End of the Great Game

By Avery Mann

A Mark Jamison Novel

First published by Dog Ear Publishing
4011 Vincennes Rd
Indianapolis, IN 46268
www.dogearpublishing.net

ISBN: 978-1-4575-3489-8

This book is printed on acid-free paper.

This book is a work of fiction. Places, events, and situations in this book are purely fictional and any resemblance to actual persons, living or dead, is coincidental.

Printed in the United States of America

AUTHOR'S NOTE

A Persona Non Grata is an unwelcome figure, usually a diplomat who has lost the favor of the host state and must be withdrawn by the sending state, commonly referred to as being PNG'd.

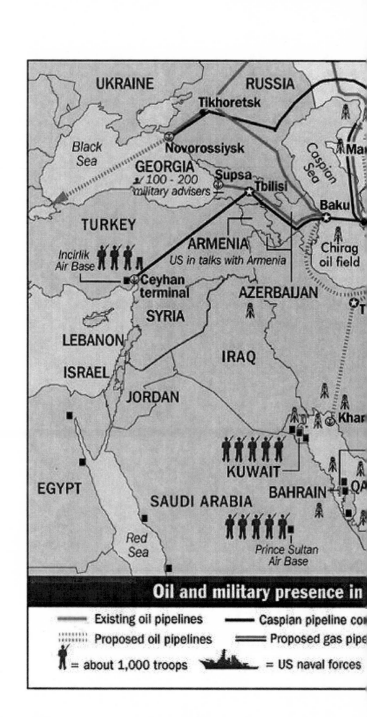

Oil and military presence in

Existing oil pipelines — Caspian pipeline co

Proposed oil pipelines === Proposed gas pipe

= about 1,000 troops = US naval forces

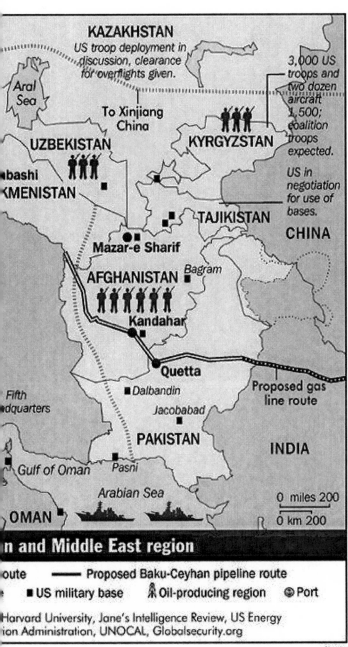

KAZAKHSTAN
US troop deployment in discussion, clearance for overflights given.

Aral Sea

To Xinjiang China

UZBEKISTAN

bashi
KMENISTAN

KYRGYZSTAN

3,000 US troops and two dozen aircraft 1,500; coalition troops expected.

US in negotiation for use of bases.

TAJIKISTAN

CHINA

Mazar-e Sharif

AFGHANISTAN *Bagram*

Kandahar

Quetta

Proposed gas line route

Dalbandin

Jacobabad

PAKISTAN

INDIA

Fifth dquarters

Gulf of Oman *Pasni*

Arabian Sea

OMAN

| 0 miles 200 |
| 0 km 200 |

n and Middle East region

oute ——— Proposed Baku-Ceyhan pipeline route

■ US military base 🎋 Oil-producing region ◉ Port

Harvard University, Jane's Intelligence Review, US Energy
ion Administration, UNOCAL, Globalsecurity.org

STAFF

INTRODUCTION

Like any other sovereign state, the Vatican has its own intelligence organization that prepares daily briefings for the pontiff and other key members of the Curia. While the Vatican's gathering service is small, it is fed from a number of larger collection sources from around the world, including those highly confidential in nature. The briefing materials contain portions that are, therefore, delineated with a security classification in the same fashion as those provided by major intelligence organizations to their respective governments. These larger agencies interface with the Vatican in an effort both to gauge reaction and test the content of the material shared and to curry favor with one of the world's greatest sources of global public influence.

Among those people shaping the Vatican's collection efforts has been one of its most distinguished residents since 1981. While no longer openly considered its most influential intellectual force, this man remains the figure most fully in possession of both the Vatican's tightly guarded internal secrets and the more dynamic world of global intelligence flows, which he continues to monitor and observe.

Cardinal Joseph Aloisius Ratzinger arrived in Rome as prefect of the Congregation for the Doctrine of Faith and resigned as Pope Benedict XVI on February 28, 2013, when he was flown by helicopter to the Papal summer residence of Castel Gondolfo, a journey he often piloted himself in his time as pope. The now-emeritus Pope Benedict returned to the cloister of the Vatican, his previous home of thirty-two years, upon the completed renovation of the Mater Ecclesia on May 2, 2013. This small monastery sits behind St. Peter's Basilica and is incorporated into the protruding Leonine wall near the Aquilone fountain in the Vatican Gardens.

From his sanctuary, Pope Benedict maintains a watchful presence over developments both within and outside this smallest of city states. He is privy to everything from the most guarded visions of the saints collected over the life of the Church of St. Peter, to the latest assessments of Islamic State movements within Syria and the surrounding region.

Then-Cardinal Ratzinger's efforts to preserve Christian doctrine found greater favor in the West of 1981 and stood in marked opposition to the communist atheism promoted by Brezhnev's Soviet Russia. Even then, he knew the true heart of Christianity to be preserved by the oppressed in such systems, as Pope John Paul came best to represent and as they both understood and fully valued.

The fall of the Berlin Wall in 1989 began a shift evident both within the Vatican and around the world. The West became the exclusive superpower and left Russia and the newly independent countries without substantial guidance or assistance as the orthodox churches once again took hold without any official opposition.

While the West turned more relativist and accepting of all points of view and practices, in the East, the Church was more responsive to preserving Christian doctrine. Both a former KGB agent and a US intelligence agent found themselves in correspondence with the Vatican and, through their contacts, directly with Cardinal Ratzinger. One was named Vladimir Putin, and the other was named Mark Jamison.

PART I

CHAPTER

1

The Vatican—April 2014

Sunlight poured over the Aquilone fountain as the water within it cascaded, reflecting light and sound through the Vatican Gardens and onto the Leonine wall behind the great Basilica of St. Peter. His pleated white cassock glowed as the illumination filled the carved mahogany side table, gently warming him and the notes being scrawled by his aging hand. He wore the brown slippers of a humble priest this morning in his upper study at the Mater Ecclesiae, no longer affording himself, even in private, the red shoes he'd relinquished with the Ring of the Fisherman. He smiled at the red and white geraniums in his window boxes, thinking of the complete control he now seemed to enjoy over his personal quarters and activities. With thanks to the Almighty, he could still play the piano—now, when the mood struck and Mozart beckoned, he could play without interruption.

On this splendid spring morning, he momentarily thought back to the dreadful exams, both written and oral, that had taken his professorial attentions on the faculty in Bonn, Munster, Tubingen, and Regensburg before he could ascend in the Church hierarchy in Germany and then Rome. It was certainly wonderful to be free from so many tasks that impinged on his devotion to God and the beauty of His Creation. He viewed life as a blossoming flower that unfolded in new and unexpected ways, yet always captured the imprint of Creation.

It had come to be that two of his most vexatious graduate theology students were now among his most devoted and relied upon assistants at the Mater Ecclesiae. Both Monsignor Bertrand Eke and Archbishop Juergen Scheuer maintained daily contact with him and continued to enable his most confidential tasks through a flow of data and analysis from discreet collections of information from around the world. Each also knew the particular variant of chess the retired pontiff enjoyed playing and sought diligently to master it.

As Monsignor Eke climbed the carpeted wooden steps to the papal study on this particular April morning, Benedict XVI thought that Eke most perfectly captured the spirit of the Vatican's old Holy Alliance, later called simply "the Entity." Forty popes had previously relied on the espionage service of the Vatican not only to collect intelligence, but to directly affect the course of history through bribery, murder, and countless layers of intrigue in the courts and salons of power. Then came Monsignor Umberto Benigni's more modern approach early in the last century. Of course, this new approach also aimed at curtailing the reformist notions of "modernist" liberal Catholics or anything else that threatened sacred dogma and the ordained guidance first enunciated by the Almighty through Jesus and Peter.

"Good morning, Bertrand."

"Good morning, Holy Father."

"So please sit and join me for a late breakfast. The parrot has already eaten and the flowers have been watered. The Sisters of Mercy have shown their mercies on us and left many baked delicacies for our enjoyment.

"Paparazzi's molt is looking better than yesterday, don't you think? He is about as green now as the rubber plant under his perch." The Pope looked at the bird, smiling, and motioned again for Father Eke to sit down.

"Thank you, your Holiness," Monsignor Eke responded as he gently hiked his black cassock up and pulled his tall, slightly stooping frame together to sit, placing his briefing box on the study table as he did so. Eke always gave a second glance toward Paparrazi, with whom he shared an aquiline nose, although Eke's nose was far more distinguished, resting under his greying hair, as he silently assured himself. "We have many developments coming from Moscow."

"You see, dear Bertrand? We were certainly right to establish a full diplomatic embassy at the Kremlin five years ago. Medvedev and now Putin are proceeding just as we'd hoped. They have taken up the mantle of the Tsars, protecting the Christians. While the West has turned its back on the Christian refugees fleeing from both the madness they unleashed in Iraq and Syria and the mess they have now ignited in Egypt and across North Africa, only Russia's relationship with the Orthodox Church has given these people reassurance. Our Catholic flocks in these countries only look to Russia now."

"Putin's former atheism is being tested, Your Grace. Politics seems to be driving him to us, as he now wears his baptismal cross. We also have several memoranda about saving the Christians of Syria."

"Bertrand, try these cakes—marzipan, your favorite. May I pour your coffee?"

"Please. Thank you."

"A thought occurred to me during my early morning walk and meditation today, Bertrand. Many of the Syrian Christians fleeing now are Armenian, and some of the most intense fighting is in Der Zor. Do you recall its significance? It's literally built on the bones of Armenians driven from their homeland. They're starving once again, being driven from their homes once again. And now we learn that even their Genocide Memorial Church, containing the remains of hundreds of thousands of their grandparents, has been blown up by the Islamic State.

"You know, we never answered their pleas and prayers before. The West made promises, but it was Russia that saved them from extinction."

"With our encouragement, Holy Father."

"To be sure. I often stop before the statue of Saint Gregory in the Sistine Chapel for a communion with his soul. He was like Peter to his people, and his entire nation became God's Christian illumination and an inspiration to pagan Rome."

"The marzipan is good. The sisters made these?"

"Actually, there is a bakery outside near the Spanish steps, though they would like to think they could make these."

"Our secret."

"Remember also, Bertrand, that we failed the Eastern Catholics and the Orthodox of Byzantium during the Crusades and again when the Turks sacked it. It was a disgrace that we allowed the center of learning, of Christian knowledge, to fall. It is true that Rome and the western Church then became the undisputed center of the Christian world, but think of what was lost. The knowledge, the treasure, the collected wisdom of the Greeks, Arabs, and Armenians—even the Egyptians. Constantinople did not become Istanbul. Constantinople was lost forever, along with its secrets, its *Liberia*."

"Holy Father, do you think the Armenians may hold a key to the *Liberia?* I understand that Putin still pretends he is trying to find it in the tunnels and chambers running under the Kremlin."

"Personally, I think the lost Byzantine collections left that area long before the fall of Constantinople. If Putin thinks Ivan the Terrible got his hands on it, let the Russians keep looking under Moscow. You know that our own Catholic Armenians on San Lazaro Island began bringing in both the sacred writings of the Armenian Church and ancient Greek and Byzantine manuscripts to preserve them from the Turks before the fall. The vaults on that island are still off limits, even to the popes. Whether it contains all of the *Liberia* or some of it, I'm certain it contains secrets— even secrets the Entity couldn't ascertain."

"Secrets as good as this baking?" Bertrand interjected with a full mouth and Cheshire smile.

"Secrets associated with the way we play chess…Shall we call it Byzantine chess? There is more to understand with this game of chess than any other I have studied.

"Let me go through the materials you have gifted me this morning. I plan to make my notes for Pope Francis and then take a short rest. Perhaps we can play our game at four o'clock and finish in time for dinner?"

The monsignor nodded in agreement, still enjoying the marzipan.

"Please invite Juergen to join us at six this evening for dinner and ask Maria to collect our treats now and share them with others. She can take the coffee tray, also. Thank you, dear Bertrand."

Monsignor Eke took his leave. As Benedict XVI prepared to read in earnest, he reflected on his place in the chain of popes. He enjoyed the rare opportunity to observe the actions of his successor. The visions of a number of saints in the history of the Church shared a common theme—that the papacy of Benedict XVI would be the next to last. Francis, according to these visions, would be the final pope, ushering in a world government, the Antichrist, and the coming of the End of Days. Benedict wasn't at all sure he was convinced that any of this would come to pass, but as he reflected upon the increasing violence and chaos in the world, he certainly hoped his stepping down didn't hasten the end of the world.

CHAPTER

2

The afternoon session of Byzantine chess afforded the former pontiff an opportunity to question Monsignor Eke about some of the reports he reviewed and to gain his insights into the goings on among the Curia. Benedict always examined the reporters as much as the reports he received. He understood that items that might give offense or upset to His Eminence were those most likely to be excluded, but those were precisely the ones he garnered the greatest interest in.

This afternoon, Eke revealed nothing except a particularly unexpected play on the unique chessboard, which took Benedict unawares.

"And where did that come from? Are you and Juergen out to defeat an old man by perfecting your mastery of arcane chess attacks such as this? You aren't being coached by the unholy one, are you? Is Lucifer showing you these moves?"

They both smiled and looked into each other's eyes with an affection that reflected a depth of shared understanding and a loyal friendship of nearly forty years.

"Do you recall how we came by this game, Bertrand?"

"Of course I do, Holy Father."

"It was all about saving the Christians in the East, wasn't it? Wasn't our source that brash American so determined to enlist our support? When did he first contact us?"

"I think it was early in 1990. Archbishop Scheuer was serving in Vienna at the time, and Jamison arranged a meeting with him through the Armenian Catholic Prelate there.

Armenians were being slaughtered again by Turks, at that time Azeri Turks in Sumgait and Baku, if I remember correctly. He reminded Juergen of our history on the subject of the massacres of our fellow Christians in the East and implored him not to let the Vatican remain indifferent this time."

"It's your move now, Bertrand."

Bertrand made his move. "It served almost to sweeten our interest when this gentleman told us there were secrets that even the Vatican and Kremlin didn't know—secrets that centered on games and ancient variations that were lost when we allowed the Turks to capture the Eastern Church. The Byzantine chess we play is only one of those that he revealed."

"You are speaking still of the *Liberia*."

"Yes, Holy Father, or rather what we believe it to be. It is more than likely that even the tsars were kept from knowledge of many of the recorded treasures that were lost or perhaps hidden all these years. Archbishop Scheuer's meeting with the American was in the Armenian complex in Vienna, and there may be some material there, although I believe more can be found with the Mekitarist Order on San Lazaro. I have heard that a collection is also in Romania, and of course in the vaults of Holy Echmiadzin near Yerevan. The Armenians also protect volumes in their quarter of Jerusalem and in Damascus. It was as if their catholicate foretold the Genocide, the ultimate destruction of its people, and took great efforts over many years to save their unique knowledge and cultural treasures.

"I spoke at some length about all this a long time ago with Catholicos Vasken, who was from Romania, and also with Cardinal Agajanian. The Church was wrong to let Byzantium fall. Whoever preserves its learning preserves the soul of all the churches."

"Bertrand, you did it to me again. Is this another move inspired by the Prince of Darkness?"

"What did you think about today's reading box? Your Grace had to be upset at seeing the destruction yet again of our faithful, as well as so many of our Muslim brothers and sisters."

"Of course, dear Bertrand—I am praying for an end to the violence, and I know Francis is doing everything possible to end the madness. Our relations with the Kremlin are more valuable than any with the West today. It's truly hard to believe there could be such a reversal of interests.

"And did you see in the summaries comments attributed to Mark Jamison? That is the American Juergen dealt with in Vienna. He seems to be reminding us of yet another series of massacres of Christians. The Egyptian Copts, the Maronites, the Syriacs, and the Armenians are completely vulnerable. The Syrian Catholics have been telling us for years that Assad is their protector, just as Iraq's Saddam protected his Christians. You knew that Tarik Aziz, Saddam's foreign minister, was a Chaldean Christian, educated in one of the English language colleges in Baghdad? I believe he was an English literature major."

Monsignor Eke confirmed the continuing value of Mark Jamison's reports before the retired Pope continued.

"Christians held prominent positions in Iraq. Many Christian Iraqi women were among the finest professionals and doctors, but the Americans seemed so indifferent to their fate. They are passionate about their friendship with the Saudis, yet claim concern for the rights of women...So much suffering, and the end is nowhere in sight."

"I'm sure Juergen will have much to contribute on this subject, Your Holiness. You were among the judges for his habilitation in Tubingen, and he has reminded me many times that you were the harshest."

"Of course. He wrote on the Eastern Church and the dilemma of the Middle Eastern Christians. I am still informed by it as a background to all that has transpired over these many years."

The retired pontiff still wasn't finished with his examination of the former student in front of him, however.

"Bertrand, your briefing materials have been discussing the riots on Taksim Square in Istanbul. On the surface, they are about whether the popular park and social meeting area will be discarded in favor of a shopping complex modeled after an Ottoman military garrison compound, but of course the real reason for the rioting, as you pointed out, is the high-handed manner in which the destruction was ordered without real public input or participation, and again, as you correctly pointed out, it is indicative of the high-handed way in which Turkish leadership behaved in the Ottoman days. What's happening now looks like a return to the old authoritarian leadership style—officials today admit their fascination, even admiration, of the old empire—so my question to you, dear Bertrand, is whether or not your research showed you the ironic background to all this."

"I'm afraid that I'm not as well informed on the historical implications of this situation as Your Grace."

"Well, Bertrand, Taksim Square was part of the grounds of the Armenian Patriarchate of Istanbul, which was confiscated without compensation while a million and a half innocents were put to death by order of the Ottoman authorities. Doesn't it give you pause to think that after all these years, there has been no acknowledgement of the horrors, and now they are adding insult to injury by constructing a replica of the military garrison compound that led the executions?"

"Ah, yes, I understand Your Grace's point entirely, but this is only consistent with the street and school names honoring the perpetrators in Istanbul and across Turkey. Even Turkish courts-martial found the Young Turks leaders guilty of the atrocities and condemned them to death, though the sentences were never carried out, and today they are still quietly honored, apparently even more so by the current leadership."

"We have been so negligent, Bertrand, so remiss in our concern for our Christian communities in the East and the continuing peril they face."

The retired Pope and the monsignor paused and sat silent.

"I thought I heard voices just now. Did Your Grace hear anything?"

"If I hear voices around here, Bertrand, its either Maria or Paparazzi—I'm afraid I'm no saint."

They both turned their faces as the entrance bell chimed below.

"Bertrand, please tell Maria to answer the door. It's probably Juergen, here to join us for dinner and grant me an excuse to end my suffering at your hands. Maybe this infernal game is the revenge of the Byzantines on the papacy!"

Maria was gone longer than expected, and Monsignor Eke went downstairs to inquire. When he arrived at the entrance, he saw that Archbishop Juergen Scheuer was standing in the doorway, accompanied by two other gentlemen. Two security officers from the Swiss Guard remained outside. One of the two visitors was introduced as Mark Jamison.

Dinner would be held up.

CHAPTER

3

They stood in the entrance hall of the Mater Ecclesia as Archbishop Juergen Scheuer introduced Mark Jamison to Monsignor Eke, who turned and dismissed Maria back to her duties. He was so confident of the reception that Benedict would offer upstairs that as she turned to leave, Eke asked Maria to prepare two extra settings for dinner.

Juergen announced that Mark Jamison was an old friend he had known since his days in Vienna, even though he knew that both the monsignor and retired pontiff were fully aware of Jamison from his reports and correspondence. Bertrand lowered his head and offered Mark Jamison his warmest welcome to the Vatican and to the Mater Ecclesia.

Jamison, in turn, introduced the black-suited gentleman who accompanied him as Constantine Popov, the personal secretary of Vladimir Putin, and Bertrand again lowered his head and spoke of his honor in welcoming the gentlemen. He invited the men to have a seat and asked if they wished to alert the retired pontiff of a reason for their unexpected visit. Jamison said to inform him that they had news from the Game Master. Archbishop Scheuer glanced at the widening blue eyes of Bertrand Eke.

"I'm sure His Holiness will be delighted to receive you both," Eke said as he pivoted and quickly ascended the steps to inform Pope Benedict of his very distinguished guests.

"The Game Master!" Benedict exclaimed at this announcement. "Are you sure he referred to the Game Master? Then he does exist! Oh my friend, this is indeed splendid. And Popov, too! Something major is afoot. There are secrets to be learned this evening!"

Archbishop Scheuer followed up the steps shortly, entering the study and looking silently at His Holiness.

"Juergen, is this Game Master something you have been working on with Jamison? Can you give me a brief word about it?"

"Holy Father, a situation is developing very quickly, and these gentlemen felt they would rather inform us together of the circumstances and the urgency that brought them to us. You know of the reliability of Jamison's reports over the years, and also of Popov's. God willing, we will all patiently discover what it is together."

"He referred specifically to the Game Master, though? You heard this as well as Bertrand?"

As Benedict finished saying this, each man opened his eyes widely, gazing into the eyes of each other.

"Yes, Holy Father. Apparently, he actually exists—and Jamison is in contact with him."

"I knew it! The Vatican first heard rumors of this Game Master as a figure responsible for attaining the release of the American hostages in Iran all the way back in January of 1981. According to the reports we received, the negotiations were inconclusive, so a strange game of chess, which we now know as Byzantine chess, was employed in the resolution. We again heard of something like this used in the bizarre dissolution of the coup against Gorbachev in '91. I even gave thought to the value of employing such a figure as this Game Master in an internal dispute among the Curia before either of you arrived at the Vatican, but there was no real evidence that such a figure existed or that resolutions of this nature were possible. The rumors that reached us, though, were enough to stir my interest in both Byzantine chess and the secrets lost from the *Liberia* of Byzantium—or maybe not lost, but just missing. Soon, this mysterious figure was being referred to regularly as the Game Master, though it was only in rumor and speculation.

"Let's have them come up to the study, and give me a few moments to prepare myself. Please offer them an aperitif…Five minutes, not more."

"As you wish, Holy Father."

Archbishop Scheuer returned downstairs to join the guests while Monsignor Eke helped tidy the study and arrange the seating for the visit. When the retired Pope emerged from the bathroom and nodded his head, Bertrand headed downstairs to invite the group up, telling them to bring their sherry glasses with them.

Benedict had planned to remain seated when the group entered his study, but was too excited to finally meet Jamison and Popov. He stood and hurried as best he could toward the doorway as they entered, warmly shaking their hands and offering his heartfelt appreciation for Jamison's and Putin's friendship and correspondence over the years.

"Mr. Popov, please pass along my warmest regards to your president and my personal friend. Although we never actually met, I feel a familial connection with him."

"President Putin assures Your Excellency of his highest respect and warmest regards. As you know, Your Holiness, President Putin feels that Russia today is the Third Rome, the legitimate successor to Byzantium. As such, he is committed to protecting the Christians of the East with Your Grace's support. He asks me to convey to you that it is Russia that is holding the line of Church doctrine against the agnostic relativism of the West."

"Such an incredible change from the Soviet atheism he once professed."

"But Your Grace must appreciate that even in the Soviet days, the light of the Orthodox Church continued to burn. True, maybe it was just flickering at times, but the total separation from the State then actually cleansed the Church of political intrigue. The mind of Russia may have endeavored to be atheist, but its soul was still illuminated by candles and icons.

"Your Holiness, President Putin also thanks you and Pope Francis for your assistance in reducing the volatility of Syria by supporting a ceasefire and the destruction of chemical weapons—as President Putin puts it, you provided the moral underpinning for his very practical diplomatic resolution—and may I also add my own appreciation to you both."

The former pontiff nodded his head and then turned to embrace Mark Jamison, who presented Benedict with two jars of fresh honey. The former pontiff knew immediately that the two men must have come directly from meetings at San Lazaro, whose monks lavished honey on special visitors.

"How very thoughtful. How are the Mekhitarist fathers? Father Mesrop, I believe, sent this."

"You continue to display your uncanny knowledge, Holy Father." Mark beamed. "Father Mesrop sends his prayerful and warmest regards."

"Tell me, my friends, where did the secrets of the *Liberia*, the ancient knowledge of Byzantine Rome and the East, go when it fell? Mr. Popov, is it hidden under Moscow as your president suspects? Mr. Jamison, did the Armenians take it to Venice? Mark, I'm beginning to suspect the abbots shared more with you over the years than just honey...And shared the same thing, perhaps, also with the Game Master?"

At this, Constantine Popov interjected, "Look, your Holiness, the Mekhitarists didn't come to Venice until the eighteenth century. How could they possibly have the *Liberia*?"

Mark added, "1715, to be exact."

"Your Grace, perhaps my studies will allow me to fill in some gaps," Archbishop Juergen Scheuer importuned.

"Please, Juergen—if the rest of you are interested. Go ahead, Juergen, please."

To everyone's astonishment, the archbishop collected a folder from among the retired pontiff's briefing materials, cleared his throat, and began to read.

"As you know, the Second Rome is the term applied to the Byzantine Empire, begun by Emperor Constantine in 330 AD when he shifted his throne eastward to escape the invasions and fragmentation preoccupying the Italian peninsula in the fourth and fifth centuries. His seat of power would be named Constantinople and would remain the dominant center of western civilization for the next 1,000 years.

"Though they were situated in Hellenic Asia Minor and gradually allowed the Greek language to supplant Latin, the Byzantines never thought of themselves as anything but true Romans and the keepers of the legacy of an empire dating back to the expansion of the Republic in the second century BC.

"Perhaps the greatest Byzantine emperor was Justinian, whose name is still so identified with enduring legal concepts and organization that we continue to refer to the totality of these as 'Justice.' Justinian was also a great leader who fought to regain much of the Roman territory that was previously lost, including wresting by conquest the Italian peninsula back from Gothic people and other occupiers by 555 AD. In this way, the preeminent Eastern Roman Empire conquered and garrisoned many of the territories of the Western Roman Empire, including Rome itself.

It was at this juncture that the Armenians entered into prominence in the West, though they had been prominent in the East since antiquity. After securing the Byzantine Empire's eastern border with the assistance of the Christian Armenians in a diplomatic resolution of the Roman-Persian Wars, Justinian's Armenian general Nerses, with an army of 35,000, turned to campaigns in northern Italy and with Byzantine general Belasarius successfully attacked resistance to Roman rule wherever it was located. Nerses remained a celebrated governor of Venice, and the historic role of the Armenians and the Veneto commenced.

"Over the centuries its role grew. Trade with the East expanded to include fleets of Armenian merchant ships plying the Mediterranean from historic Greek and Armenian lands to the new Venetian center of Western trade, commerce, industry, and banking. An Armenian Byzantine princess, Maria Argyra, became Dogaressa of Venice in 1003.

"Venetian Doge Enrico Dandolo entered into a formal trade pact with Armenia. This is the same doge who diverted members of the Fourth Crusade in 1202 to do Venice's bidding in regard to ending the economic rivalry of Constantinople. Instead of going on to conquer Muslim Egypt and retake the Christian center of Alexandria, the crusaders who were admitted through the great walls and fortifications of Constantinople en route remained to loot its treasures and to ransack and burn much of the Byzantine capital. The looting was so thorough that even the gilt bronze horses from the Hippodrome of Constantinople found their way to St. Mark's Cathedral.

"With the ruin of Constantinople, power shifted immediately to Venice, which expanded its imperial dominion eastward from Dalmatia to Cyprus and to Crete in what it called the Duchy of the Archipelago, and the importance of Cilician Armenia grew. Doge Sebastiano, who had lived there as an ambassador of Venice, left funds in 1253 for a permanent Armenian palace in Venice that is today found a short distance from San Marco Square on the Calle deligli Armeni.

"With the fall of the Armenian Kingdom of Cilicia in 1375, Armenian King Levon (Leo) V and several hundred of his staff and followers took refuge in the Serene Republic, as Venice was then known. It was more common to hear the Armenian language on the cosmopolitan lanes and canals of the Veneto than to hear English or German. In fact, in 1512, Armenian language books began being published in Venice, starting with Hakob's *Friday Book*.

"With the Ottoman siege and conquest of the greatly weakened Constantinople in 1453, the threat to the Veneto no longer came from economic rivalry with another Christian center, but from the Muslim Turks, who soon controlled the sea lanes for trade with the East and began attacking Venetian trading centers.

"Once again, Armenians became noteworthy in the Serene Republic because of this new threat. Michel Surian, an Armenian, was instrumental in assisting Pope Pius with creating the Holy League, which gathered its fleets to defeat the Turkish armada in the Battle of Lepanto in 1571, heralding the end of unrivaled Turkish supremacy in the eastern Mediterranean. At that time, however, it was the genius of Antonio Surian in naval and mechanical engineering, as well as medicine, that was credited with determining the victory.

"Working with the Arsenal of Venice, the largest industrial complex in the world at the time of the battle, Antonio Surian designed a new class of rapid-firing and accurate naval cannon and included them in his newly engineered and heavily armed galleasses, which turned the tide of battle. He also gained fame for innovations in rapid damage control, which saved ships from sinking during the battle, and for new ways to treat the wounded, which were credited with saving lives. He helped rescue many thousands of Christian slaves from the captured Turkish galleys. Antonio Surian, who was widely known simply as "the Armenian," later became the Serene Republic's ambassador to England.

"Venice's prosperity continued, though its ultimate decline was assured by Portugal's opening of sea routes to India, which ended Venice's trade monopoly. The suffering of the Armenians and other Christians under Muslim rule was unrelenting and well known in Venice and throughout the West. In 1715, twelve Armenian Catholic monks, led by Mekhitar of Sebaste, arrived in the Veneto. Two years later, they were ceded the island of San Lazaro. To its monastery, the monks of San Lazaro added a publishing house and a protected repository of classical Armenian literary treasures that had escaped continuous episodes of destruction and looting in a homeland besieged over the millennia by Persians, Seljuk Turks, Huns, Byzantines, Arabs, and Ottoman Turks.

"The Armenian monastery at San Lazaro remains, though Venice itself was conquered by Napoleon in 1797 and was incorporated into the Kingdom of Italy in 1866."

Benedict raised his eyebrows and gave a nod of satisfaction, offering an upturned smile to the archbishop. "My goodness, Juergen. I hope I scored your habilitation high enough. That was quite a presentation. May I suggest we adjourn now to the dining room before you pick up another folder? Please know there was some stretching of the soup, so it might taste a bit watery."

The retired pontiff couldn't resist adding, "You would imagine that after all these years of trying to convert water to wine, we would at least be able to stretch the soup unnoticeably. Come on then, let's eat."

CHAPTER

4

As they sat, the former pontiff looked at Monsignor Eke, who proceeded with the blessing and another word of welcome to their guests. They took their soup nearly in silence. While the next course was being served, Benedict asked the question on everyone's mind:

"Well, my friends, please inform us of what brings you here. I can only suspect the dire circumstances of these recent days in the East are at the heart of your visit."

Mark Jamison looked at Popov, who nodded to him, indicating that he could take the lead in telling the purpose of their visit.

"As Your Grace knows, the historic Great Game, as it's called, involved the British and Russian empires in a contest for domination of the Middle East and Central Asia. It resembled nothing so much as a continuing chess match of checks and occasional checkmates. This was played out using the regional leaders as players and the local people as, well, one could say pawns.

"The Crimean War was a powerful example of this: The Ottoman Turks were butchering Christian minorities, and both the British and the Russians professed their desires to help them. The British feared that the Russians would move southward if the Ottomans were defeated. So in spite of howling protests from the humanitarians in Parliament, British forces actually joined the Ottomans and attacked Russia. The delighted sultan ceded Cyprus to the British, and the slaughter of innocents continued.

"With the end of the First World War, the effort to slice and dice the Middle Eastern region was in full swing. Even while Russia was sidelined while sorting out its own revolution, Stalin managed to change several borders of territories from czarist days. This built in tensions keeping Moscow at the center as a power broker. For example, he carved up Christian Armenia and Muslim Turkic Azerbaijan in ways that made continuing friction inevitable; when things calmed down in that region, the Russians helped stir it up again. In reality, neither side in the Great Game was interested in the local areas or peoples, but used them to their own advantage and, hopefully, to the disadvantage of the other side.

"Following the Second World War, the US joined the Great Game on the British team and a new player was introduced with the creation of Israel. Resource extraction at the lowest cost became a major part of the equation—for example, creating and deepening America's relationship with Saudi Arabia.

"The Great Game hasn't gone away, but has grown considerably nastier, as evident recently in Iraq and Afghanistan, and now Syria. Even the maneuvering over the future of the Ukraine and Russia's recent annexation of Crimea are extensions of this game, and it continues without any logical basis. It was developed in the British Foreign Office a long time ago to protect the Jewel in the Crown of Empire—India—but after India's independence and the breakup of the Soviet Union, it makes no sense to see Russia and the West pull further apart, especially when both of their real interests are threatened like never before."

Popov added, "It is not only the volatility of the Middle East and the dire Chinese need for global resources—we have learned now that a new player may have emerged who threatens all modern civilizations, Western and Eastern alike."

"Please go on," directed the retired pontiff.

Jamison continued. "The situation with the Malaysian airliner that recently disappeared has been surrounded in a fog of doubletalk, probably because of the larger reality that is now being uncovered. Our sources have informed us that the airplane did not crash, but was instead secretly flown to an undisclosed location. They believe it likely that the aircraft is being outfitted with an Electro Magnetic Pulse device that, if properly engaged at a high enough altitude, could destroy all electronic systems and electric grids over a huge area, possibly as large as Europe or the United States. This would be immediately catastrophic: all nuclear reactors would quickly lose their cooling systems, military defensive measures would be neutralized, financial and health records would be lost, aircraft aloft would plummet, and ships at sea would go dead in the water. Modern land transport would cease."

"One lost plane could render so much destruction?" Pope Benedict asked.

Popov interjected, "I can tell you that we have developed EMP technology, and it works as Mark described. The Chinese have been acquiring it, as well as everything else we have developed, from the Ukrainians to avoid paying our rightful intellectual property fees. Now that we have Crimea back and Kiev wants to please Europe, let's see how the Chinese do at paying retail to us."

"Holy Father," Mark continued, "the reason for the delay in getting information from Malaysia is that their investigation turned to an inventory of their air fleets. I'm afraid it isn't just one missing airliner at this point. They can't account for a number of planes that were scheduled for maintenance or otherwise temporarily placed out of service."

"Well, how many aircraft are we speaking about?"

"There are seven unaccounted-for aircraft just from Malaysia. They could be dispersed around the world by now with new markings and transponder codes. Then, when the terrorist group called Libyan Dawn recently captured Tripoli's airport, eleven commercial airliners disappeared from the Libyan capital."

"What?" Benedict looked into the eyes of his disciples. "Wouldn't Western spy satellites have been able to track the movement of these aircraft?"

"Sadly," Jamison responded, "the satellites have to be positioned in geosynchronous orbit, and all Western eyes at the time were on the Eastern Ukraine, looking for evidence of Russian troop movements."

"And you say neither Russia nor the West was behind this?" Scheuer asked, incredulous.

"We see no evidence of Chinese involvement, either, but it is impossible to know the lengths that al Qaeda or North Korea might attempt."

"Or Chechen rebels, or Uighur separatists, or any of a hundred groups promoting armed insurrection," Popov added. "Each of our countries has its hands full dealing with domestic terrorists and those based abroad. This is why any friction between us now is completely unacceptable. If we don't pull together, these factions will pull our nations apart and bring us down. This is a challenge to our global civilization; a civilization fully shared by Russia and the West."

With another nod from Popov, Jamison continued. "With the permission of Your Holiness, something else strikes us as ridiculous in the modern context and we think must change. The continued disunity of the Christian church is also foolish in the face of these threats. When all of Christendom is under siege by relativist thinking, which weakens any spiritual underpinnings of our society, does the ancient schism of the Latin and Orthodox rites make any sense today?"

Popov quickly added, "You know President Putin's unequivocal position on this."

"We do, and we are most appreciative," Benedict immediately responded. "I know Pope Francis agrees with his entire heart. We will pray about these amazing dangers and for the unity of these important nations, and certainly for the unity of Christ's Holy Church."

As they continued to partake of their simple fare in momentary silence, Benedict and his advisers took the time to digest far more than the watery soup and the slender portions of lamb with new parsley potatoes.

"Go on, my friends, please…I do apologize for the meagerness of this dinner."

"Our compliments to your cook, your Holiness—Constantine and I are certainly aware that our visit was unexpected."

After some discussion of the former pontiff's life in retirement and how much his Chopin had improved with more time for the piano after his retirement, Juergen Scheuer asked the retired pontiff if Mark Jamison might follow up on certain other recent reports he'd sent concerning the Middle East that were also very troubling.

"Of course," Pope Benedict responded, "but only after you refill their wine glasses."

As the archbishop filled the glasses, he looked to Jamison. "Please enlighten us, Mark."

"Holy Father, we have known for some time of the risks involved with the competing plans for the Middle East—the Iranian pipeline to Latakia, Syria and the competing Saudi pipeline to Haifa, Israel. You have already seen reports of the threats made both to prevent the Syrian pipeline and to continue to isolate Iran. These are similar to the threats that were made to keep Saddam from building a pipeline that did not terminate at Haifa.

"As you doubtlessly know already, the flow of Iraqi oil and natural gas, and control of Iraq, could be at the center of a new war. Will Iraqi oil and natural gas go to Syria or to Israel? Now that the battle against the Islamic State is raging across Syria and Iraq, my sources tell me that the Kurds will not be able to hold the line. The only land army strong enough to deal with the Islamic State belongs to Turkey.

"But Turkey is opposed to an independent Kurdistan and won't fight alongside the group that aims to splinter Turkey for Kurdish independence. If Turkey enters the war on the ground, the question is whether it will ever return home or whether it plans to create a new Ottoman Empire by occupying the northern half of Syria and Iraq to defeat the Islamic State, but then to remain to control the Kurdish population and the oil found there."

"So Turkey holds the key," Scheuer interjected, "and the question is whether a country that can't come to grips with its bloody past can now be expected to deal responsibly with the entire region's future?"

Constantine Popov now felt compelled to add even more to the complexity. "Russia is convinced that funds from both Turkey and Israel are finding their way to the Islamic State. When Turkey moves to occupy the north of Syria and Iraq, Israel intends to occupy the southern half of Syria. It will be supported by Saudi Arabia. Iran would then follow by moving into southern Iraq. Russia will then be forced to commit its troops along the southern flank of the old Soviet Union, including the occupation of Azerbaijan and Nagorno Karabagh."

Popov continued, "This would only precede a larger war, in which Russia would need to maintain a balance, possibly siding with Iran against Turkey, Israel and Saudi Arabia."

Mark resumed his summary, "In short, Your Holiness, this is shaping up to be a very hot conclusion of the latest chapter of the historic Great Game."

The retired pontiff raised his right hand midway, his palm down. "And so you approach this old man for what purpose?"

"Well, Your Grace, we want to stop this madness in the same way that the bombing of Syria was stopped—by a secret intervention behind the obvious public give-and-take—and we know of your love of history and of ancient gaming secrets preserved in certain lost manuscripts. We also know that you have long suspected the clandestine role of the shadowy Game Master in resolving conflicts around the world."

"In other words, you both have not only been informing me for these many years, you have also been spying on me...Go on, please."

"Finally we know of your deep and abiding sorrow, and the sorrow of the entire Church, for the enormous suffering and loss endured by Christians of the Middle East."

"Yes."

"So we have been at work developing a proposal and plan of action. You correctly assumed that the final leg of our work was at San Lazaro with the Game Master and with scholars of classical Armenian and Greek—the language of early Armenian writing, as Your Holiness knows— and ancient Persian. We express our deepest appreciation to the Game Master and to President Putin, who has supported our efforts."

"Holy Father, we are here because we believe we can end the Great Game with an actual game, or a final series of games. The Sunni and Shia Muslim leaders we have met with are convinced that the long-term effect of Christians fleeing the Middle East is catastrophic for future stability and the inward investment needed for revitalization. They want the process reversed and are willing to act in a dramatic fashion to do so."

"Even the Israelis can see their long-term decline in the hands of right-wing Jewish nationalists. In fact, the model of a more polyglot secular entity, rather than a strongly Jewish state, has advantages in breaking the stranglehold of the right."

"We have an opportunity to perform another Russian and Vatican-brokered pacification of the Middle Eastern region using games to quickly resolve impasses that eventuate in the process of negotiation. The formula is negotiation and a kind of arbitration with an agreed recourse to game resolution."

The retired pope raised his hand again in the same fashion as before.

"Mark, you have probably been made aware of my fascination with some of the games you presented to us over my years at the Vatican, and you must know how eagerly I await learning of what you and the Game Master may have uncovered in San Lazaro."

"Your Grace, I will be delighted to share everything with you and even introduce him to you at the right time. But the proposal we place before you now is this. We want you to be one of three figures who will select the game and rules and to be one of the three agreed-upon judges. As the Pope Emeritus, you bring a great deal of credibility, knowledge, and wisdom to this process. Plus, you are considered to be someone who is among the most well-versed in music and the arts, really all aspects of Western culture, as well as imbued with a fascination for the complexities of game theory and practical applications. We know that your fascination with these matters is so great that you even taught yourself to fly the papal helicopter and earned a pilot's license at an age when others often must relinquish their precious driver's licenses."

"Constantine, your turn." The retired pontiff turned his head toward Popov.

"First, Your Holiness, please know that the Game Master is Muslim…But President Putin has had a highly secret meeting with him and places his full trust and confidence in him. Of course, this was all facilitated because of his long and close relationship with Mark Jamison.

"The Game Master shares our pain when it comes to how badly the Christians have been treated and how damaging their destruction and flight has been on that region. Over the years, Mark has made him acutely aware of the

Armenian Genocide in particular. He is horrified to now see the continued suffering, killing, and dislocation of all Christians remaining in the region—the Orthodox and other Christians who don't hold allegiance to Rome, whom the Vatican seems to have abandoned to their horrible fate. We think it is time not only for the Muslims to welcome back the Christians, but for the Western Church to welcome back the Eastern Church, and to support a rebirth. I know President Putin wants this—he wants to join you in ushering in the Third Rome."

The five men sat silent for a moment, as Benedict searched the faces of Eke and Scheuer for signs of their reactions. Each sat expressionless.

Jamison continued. "Our reason in being so bold about this plan and our approach to you is that we are willing to share with you secrets that could make the outcome of your games, well, shall we say...*predictable*. I had been discussing some of this with Archbishop Scheuer on the way over and while we'd sat together downstairs before dinner. He seems to know a great deal about Byzantine chess. The Game Master says that he looks forward to being the resource for facilitating this transformation and rebirth and to enlightening you personally in all he has discovered at San Lazaro."

"Please let an old man fully grasp what you are saying: We are discussing a series of games that could ultimately determine the future of Christianity in the Middle East and, indeed, whether the Middle East has a future at all beyond endless carnage. Is that correct?"

"It is."

"And we are discussing bringing to a close the separation of the Eastern and Western Churches and reconstituting the one true Church, the Third Rome, which would be supported by Russia and the West. An effective end to the Great Game and resolution of the schism at all levels?"

"Yes."

"Why, if these powers have been unwilling for so long to act would they join together now?"

Popov responded, "Because of what would follow from the enfolding scenario Mark has described. There can be no winner in a continuation of the Great Game because it has spun out of the control of Moscow or of Washington and London. In the smoldering ruins of the region, both sides see the inevitability of China moving in to their exclusion. And we have now the enormous challenge of a potentially weaponized air fleet with the capacity to literally shut down both our nations."

"What would become of the Church?" the retired pontiff continued with an outwardly calm concealment of his own trepidation.

"There would be Orthodox representation here, and you and a number of the Curia would be expected to relocate to Moscow."

"And Francis?"

"Let's let the games decide."

"This is a test of faith, then, beyond all reckoning. This would bring about the prophecy that I would be the penultimate pope and that Francis would be the last pope, but instead of ushering in the end of times, this would offer the rebirth of a Third Rome and a single Holy Church."

The five men sat, speechless, while Maria brought in dessert. Jamison took a deep breath and closed his eyes for a moment. In that very brief instant, his mind raced back to the beginning.

PART II

CHAPTER

5

Nairobi, Kenya—1980

He stood alone on an empty tarmac, bathed in the late afternoon sun. His pocket diary entry was July 14, 1980. A small twin-engine plane appeared overhead and circled, but did not land. He studied his watch carefully. He studied the worn condition of his single leather case resting beside him, then took out his $17.40 ticket receipt for the flight back to Nairobi. It was the appointed hour.

He stood waiting as a pride of lions walked directly toward him. He had nowhere to go or to hide. The driver had dropped him off and returned the two miles or so to the lodge at Masai Mara by now. He stared at the lions as they passed a few feet in front of him. He continued to stand and wait. Finally a car appeared that he was able to wave down. The lodge used its shortwave radio to contact the Rainbow Aviation Company, which had issued him the $34.80 roundtrip ticket. He asked to speak directly with its representative, who assured him that the plane had landed, but no passenger was to be found.

The gentleman explained he had to return to work at the embassy in the morning and needed a flight back. He was told that nothing else was scheduled, so he asked for any available aircraft belonging to them to come immediately and pick him up. He was told the only thing available was a large four-engine cargo plane, which he said would do just fine. The representative told him it would need to be a charter, and it would cost $3,200. The gentleman said that would be fine, as well. He had his receipt for a contract of carriage which the company would need to honor. He was told he would need to pay for the charter in cash. He replied that he had paid for his original ticket in cash.

The lodge transportation returned him and his worn leather case to the now darkening tarmac and left him once again, but this time a large plane, some sort of updated DC-3, landed and its door opened, revealing a stunning English girl about his age with short-cropped auburn hair and wonderfully large, inviting green eyes. She flashed a great smile and asked, "Just you?" He smiled back and sniffed the wonderful scent of African adventure escaping the pores of her lovely neck and throat. "Just me."

He climbed aboard, strapped in to the copilot's seat, and they took off and headed skyward. He found the combination of her scent, the heat, the intimacy of the two of them in the cockpit, and her control of the large craft overpowering. He unfastened his shoulder harness to stretch a bit and found himself staring at her.

"What?" she inquired, looking into his eyes and reading whatever message they revealed. Her smile was enchanting.

He reached over to her with a gentle kiss that brushed her lips and sucked in her perfume. She turned briefly toward him, and the delights of kissing as the French kissed accompanied the climb of both the plane and his maleness. While giving herself freely to him, she made sure to crane for glimpses at the controls and the last reflections of faded light on the difficult terrain ahead. "It's the escarpment," she explained as she broke away from him. "We don't have enough altitude."

Then everything was plunged into darkness. She could see neither gauges and controls nor the gigantic cliff she knew they were fast approaching head on. "Quick," she exclaimed, "find a torch somewhere—a flashlight, a lighter, anything. Search the cargo area." He felt his way back as she

yoke as far into her as possible. He heard the
moaning louder than they had been a few moments
e.

He somehow found a flashlight and shined it on the
controls as she directed. They held their breath as the Great
Escarpment refracted the glow of early moonlight. They
weren't going to clear the top. She cursed and pulled as
hard as she could on the yoke while ramming the throttles
even further against their stops.

"Christ! Hang on and pray," she barked.

He remained motionless as the plane roared into the
darkness. Finally, he felt it nearly scrape the treetops along
the rim as she cleared it with a flourish of relief. "So, what do
you think of this bush pilot?" He could hear her normal
voice returning and loved the enveloping sense of calm
relief they shared. He was, for the first time in his life,
speechless. All he wanted right then was to enter her hard
and continue the ride of his lifetime, but she was on the
radio and fast approaching the field.

"You know, they are going to have a reception commit-
tee of goons waiting for you. They are going to get $3,200
from you; you'd better pay them immediately. They are not
nice people, Mark."

She was trying to warn him, but all he could think
about was her deliciousness and the fact that they'd made it
back safely. He didn't even know her name. Before he could
undue his harness, she'd disappeared out of the plane.

The goons she predicted were in the doorway of the
airplane. "You can't leave until you pay the money."

He finally talked his way into getting as far as their office
before paying. They had a policeman waiting there, an even
bigger goon, who threatened, "You pay, or I take you now to
jail." Mark explained his side of the matter once again and
finally felt compelled to produce his diplomatic passport.

"You can't arrest me because I have diplomatic immu-
nity." The policeman held the passport upside down and

stared at it for a while before announcing, "We go to ja now." Mark actually felt some relief that the fellow hadn't eaten the passport, as Jamison managed to free it from his enormous hands. They were in a standoff that wasn't going very well for the American lawyer's argument concerning contractual performance on a $17.40 one-way ticket.

It was now seriously late at night, and Mark was anxious to get back to his hotel, clean up, have dinner, and get some rest. Any thoughts of his lovely bush pilot were about gone by the time another ex-patriate British pilot strutted through the office. Mark stopped him and told his story, hoping that the British pilot would understand his plight. This pilot looked at the three company men and decreed that Mark was telling the truth. He had heard other stories of the assigned pilot for the original flight not bothering to land for single passengers from the Mara. The pilot used his commanding presence to order the representatives to accept the ticket as full payment, apologize for holding Mark up for the past few hours, and immediately arrange a taxi to get him back to the Nairobi Hilton.

Victory!

The next morning, Mark regaled his colleagues with the tale and dutifully listened to a uniformly dreadful series of cases of diplomats from several other embassies who failed to be picked up on time or suffered some other form of abuse at the hands of Rainbow Aviation. Back in his office, Mark took a call from the airline, during which its manager demanded the immediate payment of $3,200 for the special charter. When told of the ex-patriate pilot who resolved the matter, the manager denied any knowledge of him or the resolution, then personally threatened Mark.

Jamison said he would call him back in the afternoon and immediately set about cancelling all contracts of the company with US agencies, with other embassies he had been working with and with the UN agencies. He replaced

...ation with a reputable local outfit that was . by his colleagues.

..ie never heard again from either Rainbow Aviation or, ..nfortunately, the lovely pilot who got him back to Nairobi alive and smiling. After a few days, he concluded that she'd abandoned him in his lurch with the goons, which made it easier to erase all thoughts of her, pleasant as they had been.

CHAPTER

6

Mark Jamison was settling in. He loved being called *bwana* and was past his rocky arrival a few weeks earlier. The embassy driver had been dutifully awaiting him at the airport that morning, holding a signboard with his name on it, and asked if he preferred to go first to his hotel or to the office. He replied the latter, which was wise, as it turned out. Upon being shown to his office, he was surprised to find another gentleman seated behind his desk.

"I'm sorry. They'd told me this was to be my office."

"Sit down, Mark. I'm the ambassador, and we have a lot of work to do."

As it turned out, at that time Jamison was the only available lawyer for the US government in East Africa. Everyone else seemed to have gone to hospital or vacation or had been temporarily recalled to other posts. Mark delighted in the attentiveness the diplomats gave to his every word—his legal approval meant that their fannies, and their careers, were not so exposed if things went awry.

The first unsettling part of his initial day at the embassy started with the driver's comment on the way in from the airport: He pointed to a particular spot along the road and told Mark that the last arrival from Washington was killed there a week before. The other embassy car and driver were forced to pull over, and the driver, a local, knew to immediately get out of the car. The female diplomat, probably fearing kidnapping and rape, locked the doors and stayed put, despite the efforts the armed assailants made into getting her out of the car. "Well, what happened?" Mark inquired.

The driver said they shot her through the window, dragged her body to the curb, and drove away. "They were stealing the car," he explained.

The second unwelcome note came at lunch that first day. Some colleagues took him along to an Indian curry spot not far away. At the restaurant, their good conversation was interrupted by a loud thud coming from the booth directly opposite. An Indian gentleman, who had been perspiring profusely during his meal, fell face down with a *wallop* on the table. The others from the embassy gave little pause in the conversation, apparently unconcerned as first the waiter, then the manager came to the Indian man's table. Finally, a white table cloth was politely draped over the man and the manager announced to all, "Nothing to be concerned about; he's dead."

But now Mark was strutting his stuff, and taking calls from ambassadors such as the one who identified himself simply as Jack in Uganda. In this case, Idi Amin had fled Uganda the previous year and the US was trying to get humanitarian assistance into the area in spite of the supplies often being stolen from Kampaala's airfield. One of the calls Mark handled related to the latitude Jack had to negotiate with the bandits. "You can't pay US dollars to them," Mark explained, "but some of the cargo they've hijacked could be 'lost.'"

The Iranian hostage crisis was in its eighth month and would have another six months to play out. Iran seemed a long way from Kenya, though. Aside from dealing with the continuing mess in Uganda, Mark thought that things in Kenya were actually quite lovely.

Tossing out Rainbow Aviation had made him very popular. On one particularly sunny morning, with the Jacarandas in bloom and the parrots and Rollers proudly displaying their yellow plumage, a young African-American diplomat came to him on a personal matter: He wanted to marry a local Kikuyu woman and had already met with her family and the tribal elders, but was worried that he might have to leave her behind when he was transferred. Jamison was delighted to help and explained the associated legalities and requirements for bringing her with him when he transferred stateside.

After some further informal hallway visits, during which the young man looked more and more alternatively perplexed and saddened, he approached Jamison formally once again.

"They're demanding a bride price that is more than I can pay. They want me to buy the tribe three cows, which are over a thousand dollars each. I offered two, and they wouldn't accept it."

The next thing he knew, Mark had volunteered to negotiate a bride price with the Kikuyu elders, who proved to be a determined lot. The impasse was breached after two meetings with the tribal council. They agreed upon an unheard-of settlement: two cows and a goat. Along with the resolution came Mark's appointment as the best man with various officiating functions.

On the big day, Jamison was tasked with carving meat from the shoulder of a roasted animal—another unfortunate goat, actually—and feeding parts of it into the mouths of bride and groom with his hands. He was also to be the first to drink from the communal bowl of ceremonial gruel, which he then passed to the bride and groom. It was a joyful occasion for all, turning more so as the bonfire was lit, the drums were beaten, and the best man was surrounded by ululating attendants. When the drumming reached a vigorous tempo, the women began jumping in unison high into the air. Jamison was gathered tightly in the center of the circle, and he soon found himself unable to move and being blissfully propelled aloft on the force of many heaving, undulating bosoms, accompanied by shrieks of joy.

Another source of pleasure during his time at the embassy was the friendship he established with a British expatriate and kindred spirit named Ted Todd. He noticed Ted dining alone at the Norfolk Hotel one evening and suggested he join Mark for dinner. Jamison wanted to impress him with the Swahili he was picking up, so he ordered as best he could in the native language. He ordered a ubiquitous side dish that mostly resembled a ball of mashed potatoes stuffed with peas and carrots. It looked precisely like what he concocted as a child playing with his food. He had listened carefully when others ordered it and followed suit. "I would like *Ndovu* on the side."

The waiter looked confused. "*Ndovu?*"

"Yes, please. *Ndovu.*"

The waiter laughed and shouted across the staid and placid premises, "He wants to eat *Ndovu!*" Smiles and laughter were heard all round.

"Well, what's so funny about that?"

"*Ndovu* means elephant."

"Okay then, what do you call the ball of mashed potatoes with peas and carrots?"

"That's *Ndovu!*" Try as he might, Jamison couldn't find a distinction between the sounds of these words.

This sort of thing went on until Mark dropped any pretense of ordering in the language for fear of what he might be served, despite a highly developed linguistic familiarity acquired through years of watching *Rama of the Jungle* on TV in his childhood. *Jambo Bwana* or *Jambo Memsab* would be about it for his forays into Swahili thereafter.

His new friend Ted worked as a financial manager for Kenyan Airlines, had a car, a membership at the Nairobi Club, and an interest in good food, classical music, and all things more adventurous than columns of figures and balance sheets. They would often trek off to Lake Naivasha, where Jamison enjoyed photographing the flamingos. Thousands stood just beyond a good camera shot, so he would move closer and try to refocus. After finding himself up to his ankles in their deposits, he realized that every step he took to get closer would be matched with a step away from him by all the ever-watchful birds.

Sunday often brought with it a drive to the Utalii College, a marvelous culinary and hospitality school situated adjacent to cliffs that drop two miles to the floor of the Great Rift Valley. After feasting affordably at the school restaurant, they would amble slowly to sit on the edge of the cliffs, their feet dangling over swaying yellow stalks that were giraffes and the moving brown shapes that identified herds of wildebeest below. They normally feasted so well that movement from this glorious spot was impossible once they sat down, even if they could imagine a better one to enjoy.

After heading back to Nairobi late on one of these Sunday evenings, they made the decision to stop for cognacs at the Nairobi Club. They sat near the old grandfather clock in the small gentleman's lounge adjacent to the massive carved-mahogany bar. Three fellows were seated at the nearby chess table in rapt concentration. A fourth, very dark-haired gentleman with a pronounced Middle Eastern look sat beside them, looking down and very troubled. Otherwise, the club was empty on this night besides a few tired staff in starched white coats and black ties. The silence and Courvosier were wonderful as Mark and Ted listened to the swinging ticks of the clock pendulum, which struck them both as slow and loud. None of the chess group spoke, and the unfortunate gentleman seated beside them looked as if he were going to retch at any moment.

CHAPTER

7

The evening was drawing late at the Nairobi Club as Mark and Ted slowly swirled and sipped the Courvosier and watched the enfolding drama of concentration in silence at the chess table. The faces of the players at the table were not visible—their eyes were trained downward, penetrating into the board. The only face they could see was the sad countenance of the fourth fellow staring toward the floor.

In the chess game, there was a move and a capture, followed by another, and then another capture. One of the players uttered a phrase in a foreign language, and then there was another play and another capture. Mark understood the words, though they were not in any language he anticipated. He looked at Ted and whispered, "Armenian. The fellow is speaking Armenian."

"What's he saying?"

"*Soude, amen ban soude*—'Lies, all lies.' He is saying the other fellow's moves were lying to him. He was deceived. It looks like this fellow is about to lose."

"So, how do you know the language?"

Mark and Ted were still whispering.

"Mother's side of the family—Genocide survivors."

Then suddenly Jamison heard another sound he thought he recognized. "Let's stay till they wind it up. I want to meet these fellows."

He heard the sound again. The player with his back to Mark and Ted was clearly besting the efforts of the Armenian, who was now visible to them and looking decidedly uncomfortable. The sound was a kind of chuckling laughter from the player facing away from them. Mark thought he had heard it a long while before this evening and his hopes about the fellow's identity were growing.

When the game concluded and the victorious player turned in Mark's direction, they caught each other's eyes and locked stares for the briefest moment. Mark was about to leap to his feet and rush to embrace this fellow when the gentleman quickly turned away, ignoring Mark entirely. He quickly exited with the Armenian and the third player, who looked to be Oriental. The despondent Middle Eastern fellow followed close behind.

"Did you recognize that fellow, Mark?" Ted inquired.

"Sure thought I did—an old friend from college days. That laugh and his appearance sure reminded me of him...Must be wishful thinking. Come on. We'd better clear out of here."

On the drive from the Nairobi Club to the Hilton that night, Mark regaled Ted with stories of his college days and the person brought to mind by that unique laughter and appearance of the chess player.

Jamison first met Hani Waladoon in the New Men's Dorm at the American University of Beirut in 1970. Hani believed in Jinn, in making the finest cardamom Arabian coffee, and in continuing his enjoyment of women by sampling the joys of representatives of all nations, even though his brother-in-law had gifted him a woman following Hani's ritual circumcision at the age of fourteen. He was also exceptionally brilliant. Mark took an immediate fancy to him because he captured so much of the Orient and its fascination with things Occidental. And because he had the most irresistible laugh and charm, even through half-inch thick glasses.

Waladoon was from Zanzibar's Pemba Island and had a lineage that literally went back to Sinbad the Sailor. Though the archipelago was located off the coast of East Africa, Zanzibar's rulers came from Oman on the Arabian Peninsula.

Oman's Sultan Seyyid Said moved his capital from Muscat to Zanzibar City in 1840 and promptly sold most of its inhabitants into slavery. Zanzibar became the center of the Arab slave trade until it was established as a protectorate of the British in 1897. By then it had a plantation and mercantile economy, the former centered on the production of cloves and the latter a product of an Indian merchant class. Unlike Zanzibar, slavery persisted in Oman until it was abolished in 1970, when the center of the Arab slave trade shifted to Mauritania, which didn't abolish the unfortunate practice until 2007.

As university students, Mark and Hani adventured together from Beirut to Istanbul and back, collecting trophy pins of conquests for Hani's map along the way. Mostly they laughed as each told stories of lives that fascinated the other.

Mark related one particularly memorable tale to Ted on the drive back to the Nairobi Hilton. Together, Mark and Hani rescued an attractive young American woman who was suffering from acute appendicitis on a crowded bus going over Turkey's Cilician Gates in the dead of a winter's night. Every time she had to leave the bus to relieve her cramping and retch, the passengers shouted for the driver to leave her there in the desolate mountains. The two took charge of her protection, one staying inside and holding the door while the other protected her privacy outside. Getting her to hospital involved horse-drawn carriages and a hired minivan in Iskenderun—the crew of which promptly robbed them and stole their luggage. They ended up walking her across a mined frontier into Syria to get her help.

The welcoming border guard rang up the world's fastest taxi driver, who met them in a heavily muscled white Dodge V-8 with over 400 horses under its bonnet. The driver sported an enormous black mole on his right earlobe, which caught Mark's attention more than once as he raced them all on credit to the American University Hospital in Beirut, some 200 miles away from where he met them. They must have set a land speed record from Latakia down the Levantine coast. She proceeded immediately into surgery while Mark and Hani came up with the funds to pay the harrowing heroic driver.

Mark also told Ted about the Zanzibar Revolution of 1963, which overthrew the Arab dynasty and its British protection, abruptly ending the luxuries of Hani's youth. Wholesale massacres of Arabs ensued. With independence and the election of a president named Karume came nationalization of Arab land holdings, visits from the Chinese, and a sharp political swing away from the West. A year later, Tanganyika and Zanzibar merged to create Tanzania under the socialist leadership of Julius Nyerere.

Mark had been involved in government service since his last year in high school, but permission for his study in the Middle East had been denied because of his security clearance. Since he had a full scholarship from Berkeley and was fully prepared for a year abroad, he went ahead and departed anyway, volunteering his services at the embassy, which requested and promptly received permission for him to remain in the region. The political staff was delighted to enlist his fresh perspective and youthful eagerness, and they were delighted to learn of his friendship with Hani Waladoon.

By the time Mark met him, Hani was already known as something of a chess master. Hani also spoke of knowing the African board game of Bao, and even the Chinese game of Go. Apparently he also knew a great deal about the political upheavals then occurring in East Africa, that the US Embassy appeared keen to know more about.

When the time came for Mark to head back to Berkeley, he hoped that he would see Hani again, but he suspected he never would. Mark was in the United States two years later when he learned that Karume, then the Tanzanian vice president, was assassinated in Zanzibar City while playing a game of Bao. The news reports indicated that

Marxists killed him because he frustrated their efforts to enlist Soviet cooperation with the nonaligned country.

Mark finished his story about his old friend Hani just as Ted pulled up in front of the Nairobi Hilton. They bid each other a good night and Ted headed home. Mark returned to his room and got ready for bed. He had enjoyed a great day and was truly grateful for Ted's friendship.

The sound of that gentleman's unique laughter back at the Nairobi Club continued to play on Mark as he drifted off to sleep. He was roused with a soft knocking at the door. He carefully opened it a few inches and peered into the hallway, but saw no one. Then he heard his name whispered very gently and pushed the door open fully. There in front of him, beaming, stood Hani.

The two embraced, and Mark pulled him inside his room and closed the door quietly behind him.

"It *was* you at the Nairobi Club. No one else could laugh like you," Mark proclaimed. They kissed each other on both cheeks and hugged again.

"Mark, I couldn't speak to you back there, but I had to see you. What brings you here?"

Mark explained his assignment at the embassy. Hani responded by saying he was visiting friends for a few days and would be heading out the following day for Muscat, where he was advising Oman's Sultan Qaboos.

Since Mark would also soon be heading there to put a technical assistance agreement in place for the United States, they agreed to meet there.

CHAPTER

8

Muscat, Oman—1980

When he arrived at the al Falaj Hotel in Muscat, Jamison was excited to finally be able to use the Arabic he acquired while living in Beirut, so he spoke repeatedly to those at the front desk, who showed no understanding of his words at all. He realized there were many dialects, but still found it strange to find no comprehension. Finally, the night clerks looked at him and asked if he knew any English. They explained that they were Pakistani guest workers who were still new in the country themselves.

As it turned out, finding an actual Omani proved challenging and then puzzling. Oman was a country of foreigners. He had his government meetings with real Omanis, and then was surprised to see all of the officials he'd met with earlier in the day standing at his hotel room door very late in the evening. Mark got out of bed. He was stunned at the sight, but invited them in as he slipped on a bathrobe.

"You honor me with your thoughtful visit," he said in his best Arabic, pleased it came out straight. Yet again, there was no response—not even a slight smile.

"Please sit down." He pointed to his two chairs and his bed, but the officials were ten in number. All remained standing, expressionless.

"May I offer you some of my cookies?" he added, his mind racing for some reason that these men would be there, staring coldly at him. His offer brought forth actual scowls from them.

He was struck by the thought that he should offer them alcoholic beverages, but thought of the possibility that this Muslim country was dry. He knew that some dry countries permit hotels to serve alcohol to foreign guests, but the offer of alcohol could also prove insulting to them if he was wrong. He took a deep breath and asked in his best English, "Johnnie Walker?" Their instant reply was, "Black Label?" The officials quickly changed their demeanor. He nodded his head in agreement and phoned room service for two bottles and a dozen glasses, which they promised to bring up right away.

His later experience working in Yemen shed light on this regional beverage of choice. Yemeni officials would chew mouthfuls of qat during meetings, occasionally taking swigs of Scotch whiskey directly from an open bottle kept on the floor beside their desks. Apparently, the qat was a stimulant and the whiskey a depressant, which kept them seated during the entire systemic gyration.

Yemen also had the remarkable feature of crews of Chinese coolies building mountainous roadways, looking like the crews that blasted and pick-axed the railways through California's high Sierra over a century and a half ago— China had nothing to offer but the labor of thousands of men. When mishaps killed the workers, the Yemenis wouldn't permit their burial in Muslim soil. China didn't have the funds to bring the bodies home, so they were buried in the roadbeds and paved over. A shrine stood beside the road to mark the burial spots. Some steep, curving mountain passes were accompanied by dozens of such shrines.

Mark particularly enjoyed Oman because it was still closed to tourism at that time. He met with the US ambassador in a building resembling a small castle above the harbor, and he went out in Land Rovers to remote areas that remained unchanged from biblical times. At one oasis town, he watched a camel sale in progress and

observed that everyone wore their wealth in gold orna-
mentation. He tracked down a gold souk where trading was
vigorous. Watching a seller weigh the gold in this most
remote spot, he saw that the weights employed were silver
coins and asked to examine one. It was a silver Maria
Theresa Thaler from Vienna, minted and stamped in 1763.

"I don't want to buy your gold, but would like some of
these weights as souvenirs of my visit. How much for each?"

The seller wrote down a number in local currency, and
Mark calculated the amount written down as $12.50 US
each, quickly checked the amount of money in his wallet,
and bought ten of the rare antique coins with a sense of
delight in finding this treasure. The oasis was very removed
from the modern world, and the use of these old coins as
simple scale weights left him satisfied he would return with
a lot more than souvenirs.

News travelled slowly to Oman, and the news that did
reach Oman that day was about the continuing hostage crisis involving those American diplomats kidnapped and con-
fined in Iran. There wasn't any real sign of progress toward
securing their release.

Jamison's work in Oman led him to conclude that the
British still controlled goods and services reaching the country and that to put a US assistance package in place would
require purchases of US source goods. He also discovered
that the Omani officials were moonlighting as import agents
and taking a fee from the British suppliers, which meant
that the US Foreign Corrupt Practices Act would put a US
supplier in legal jeopardy if it used a mandated local agent
who was also part of the government administration.

Using his best diplomatic skills by day and drafting
skills by night, he worked late into the evenings drafting an
entirely new Omani procurement code and then lobbied
for this new code during the day, using US assistance as
leverage to end what amounted to a long-standing British
monopoly. He received the State Department's Meritorious

Honor Award for pulling it off. Fortunately for Mark, the British ambassador was none-the-wiser until after his departure—he had been looking forward to a respite in London before returning to the United States.

The entire time he was working in Oman, Mark hoped to hear from Hani Waladoon. Hani remained something of a mystery to people there. He had no official standing with any agency or with the government of Sultan Qaboos, but rumors surfaced about a negotiator based in Oman who was involved with the new Islamic Republic of Iran.

9

One day while Jamison was updating American Ambassador Malcolm Wyle about progress on the technical assistance agreement, Wyle announced a surprise waiting for him in the conference room adjoining the ambassador's office. Wyle assured him the room was secure and reminded him that anything said in the room should never leave it.

Stepping inside, Jamison saw Hani Waladoon beaming his giant grin. Hani threw open his arms upon seeing his friend, and Mark crossed the room to embrace him.

"So, you know Amassador Wyle?" Mark inquired.

"Mark, I know a lot of people, although very few really know me. I'd like you to be one of those few."

"I would be honored, Hani. Does this have to do with why you couldn't acknowledge me back at the Nairobi Club? What was that all about?"

"Okay, Mark, that's as good a place to start as any. Two of the folks with me that night were Haidar Fusilev and Tigran Petoian. Ever hear of either of them?"

"No."

"They are the chess champions of Azerbaijan and Armenia, which were both seeking a means to reach a negotiation. My role was to oversee a match involving both and to play the winner. If I prevailed, I would be able to set the terms for that negotiation. Sometimes I'm even allowed to resolve a conflict in this way. You might say that the parties bring me in to decide what they can't decide for themselves for various reasons."

"That's fantastic! You mean your chess is that good?"

"Sometimes it isn't chess that we play—or at least chess as you might think of it—but whatever game is played, everything involving my participation is kept in total confidence. The Azeri people will never learn that their undefeated chess champion was defeated by Petoian; they will certainly never know that both chess champions were defeated by me. The champions know, though, and so do their governments, or whatever parties sent them to Nairobi."

"Who was the Chinese-looking fellow?"

"Ah, Li Jihua…Mr. Li. He is very interested in what I'm doing."

"Are you working for Sultan Qaboos here in Oman, or for any other country while here in Oman?"

"I work for whoever hires me, providing that I agree to work for them. Think of me as a very well-paid private contractor—a neutral arbitrator, if you like."

"How long have you been doing this?"

"Well…First, tell me about yourself."

"Compared to what you just told me, there is little to say. I'm still single, I live mostly out of suitcases, and I provide legal help mostly to the US Agency for International Development. I got interested in all this when we were studying back at the American University of Beirut. Do you remember our trip to Istanbul? Our work with the US Embassy there? There were so many great memories. We accomplished a lot, and we sure enjoyed it all…But tell me, Hani, how do you know Ambassador Wyle? Are you working for us again, too?"

"Just exploring how I might help with your hostage problem. I have many friends in Iran, and some with the Revolutionary Council. You know how passionate they are about chess. I think there may be something I can offer."

"Of course," Mark reflected. Chess, it seems, had origins in India and Persia. The Persians were both passionate about it and devoted to it. After purging itself of its shah, who was widely regarded as a product of CIA Director Allen Dulles's handiwork, the Iranians did not have the ability to reconstruct the kind of secular democracy they'd enjoyed under Mohammed Mosaddegh. Mosaddegh, a Western-trained modernist, had the temerity to seek for his country a higher percentage of the oil revenues coming from the Anglo-Iranian Oil Company and related businesses. Rather than negotiate a reasonable accommodation, the British and American companies went to Allen Dulles and demanded Mosaddegh's ouster. The campaign to discredit this highly popular and honest head of state was as ugly as it was successful, and a shah was put in his place. Therefore, at the end of the shah's regime, the Persians looked inward to their religion in an effort to regain their identity and cleanse themselves from their long suffering due to foreign manipulation. Chess was part of their history and culture and a competitive language they understood and trusted.

"What other games have you employed in this negotiation tactic?"

"It's usually determined by the local culture; it has to be something both sides feel comfortable with. You actually got me involved in Tanzania, you know. There we played Bao la Kiswahili. It proved to be the end of Karume—the game decided he had to go. He wanted to intervene in the process, and he died trying, as you might remember."

"Hani, I tried to forget all about that situation. I didn't learn about the outcome of the conflict until I was back in the United States."

"Better for you...Sure."

"I should have remembered you and your words when a bunch of Omani officials came to my room a few weeks ago. I couldn't imagine why good Muslims would want to drink alcohol. What was I thinking? Whenever you and I had wine with dinner, you would pour out the first drop and toss it on the floor. 'Not one drop shall touch thy lips,' you would quote from the Holy Koran before pronouncing, 'and this is the one drop.'

I'll bet the games reveal more than just how cultures choose to amuse themselves. Maybe they could shed more light on how they choose to think of themselves and interact with their people and the world."

"Mark, your ambassador was suggesting the same thing earlier today. We are both having dinner with him this evening, and I'll share what I know. You'd better get back to him; I'll slip out the back. Invisible people shouldn't show up at foreign embassies."

CHAPTER

10

"Bao was my first game growing up on Pemba Island—Bao la Kiswahili," Hani explained. "Bao la Kiswahili is one of the most complex and fastest moving games there is. Since my brother-in-law was the sultan, my instruction came from masters. When I showed an aptitude for it, my instruction became more intense. Abdulrahim Masoud, the bao master of Zanzibar, became my personal tutor. "

Ambassador Wyle added, "Bao la Kiswahili is studied seriously in the West in the context of game theory, complexity theory, and human psychology. I once read a Ph.D. dissertation that described the game in the context of discovering the limits of the human mind. An Agency briefing talked about Co-evolutionary Particle Swarm Optimization, whatever the hell that means, in relation to the game."

Hani smiled and continued. "You should both appreciate that one side is called North and the other South. Mark, as an AID lawyer, you would also be interested in knowing that the notion of sowing seeds is fundamentally what the game is about—sowing and capturing seeds on a board with thirty-two pits carved in four rows. You sow your own seeds, capture your opponents', and proceed, sometimes clockwise, sometimes counterclockwise. Even as fast paced as the game is, it can still take many hours to complete."

Malcolm Wyle again had something to add: "Julius Nyrere, Tanzania's first president, often said it was bao that taught him the strategies needed to defeat British colonial rule. Sometimes players have to tactically think seven moves ahead to maneuver the game in their favor. Don't forget, also, that one of Zanzibar's leaders was assassinated while playing the game."

Hani and Mark said nothing and avoided looking at each other or at the ambassador.

"Bao is also played here in Oman, where it's better known as the Hawalis game. I've obviously become fascinated by it."

Wyle next asked Hani about how he became involved in chess.

"Malcolm, would you believe when I was seven? It was also a popular game in Zanzibar, particularly enjoyed by some of the Persian and Armenian merchants who were close to my family and the sultan. Sembat Papazian heard about my skill at bao and taught me chess with a beautiful ivory set he gave to the sultan for me. When I showed some proficiency at the game, a number of older boys from Iran and even Russia showed up to play me. Those were great days, and we had lots of fun together, which continued until I was eleven or so and began playing Tigran Kiragosian, who later became a world champion. We continued to play even after the revolution in my country and my studies in Oman and England. We were still playing when I met you in Beirut, Mark."

Ambassador Wyle's household staff was headed by an African gentleman named Jama Bodeli, who carefully refilled the sherry glasses of the ambassador and his guests as they all talked. Jama studied Hani's face carefully as he did so.

The three enjoyed a fine dinner. The wine was a nice Bordeaux Wyle selected from the small diplomatic commissary at Muscat when he first reported to this post two years before. It was now properly aged, settled, and enjoyed.

During the relaxed conversation, Mark asked again how Hani came to know the ambassador. Wyle looked at Mark and said that they were old friends. It rang particularly false to Mark's ears, but he was savvy enough to know to drop the questioning.

Mark instead asked if Wyle had any news about progress toward getting the Iran hostages released after over a year of captivity. Malcolm looked down at his food for a moment and didn't answer. Mark shot a quick look at Hani, who was doing the same thing. So, Hani's presence here did have something to do with the hostage negotiations. He could hear it as plainly as if Wyle had said it aloud. Mark knew he'd better redirect the discussion to a safer subject.

"So, Hani, I understand there are many variations of chess played around the world. Is there any one of them that particularly fascinates you?"

"Ever hear of Byzantine chess?"

"No," Mark informed him. "What is it?"

The ambassador's curiosity also looked piqued. "I've played chess for years and never heard of any such thing."

"Nonetheless", Hani assured him, "It exists, and it is most remarkable. It's at least a thousand years old, a variant of Shatranj. The oldest game of Byzantine chess is Chaturanga, originating from the mists of time in India. Chaturanga was written about in the Babylonian Talmud in 300AD and was probably played long before that. It uses the chessboard you are familiar with and employs elephants and soldiers instead of bishops and pawns—and, of course, the central figure is a shah, not a king.

"Shatranj is quite different than what you are used to, though, and is very exciting. It came from Persia in the seventh century and became very popular among the Byzantines, hence the name 'Byzantine chess.' The board is nothing like what you might imagine. It is circular...It is made of four concentric rings, to be more precise. Each ring has sixteen squares. It's like playing on the surface of a cylinder.

"In addition to the Byzantines, Ala'addin, the chess adviser to Timur of Samarkand in 1400, played it. The Greeks picked it up and called it Zatrikion.

"Wars were won and lost using this game. It wasn't a game, the way you might think of it today, but more like a university education in strategy and tactics. Timur was trained in polo, horsemanship, and chess. The Byzantines knew its value, and because of this, they safeguarded some key aspects of it."

This information was new to both of the other gentlemen. They ate their quail, brown rice, and green beans quietly, in rapt attention, while Hani continued.

"I have sought to master all aspects of chess. Byzantine chess remains a great challenge to me because while the rules survive, its theory did not. I mean, the key to it seems to have been lost with the fall of Constantinople. I am convinced that this key will unlock a sequence of moves that will literally unravel the opponent. The Byzantine monks locked this up, and well they should have. The Turks didn't stop at Constantinople, as you know, and went all the way to the gates of Vienna, confident they would next take Rome, itself—but they went without the key."

"What do you think happened to it?" Mark asked Hani.

Malcolm Wyle took a shot at answering. "Probably where all their most guarded secrets went—somewhere the Turks would never be able to seize or destroy it. There are a lot of theories; the Russians think Ivan the Terrible took it. Your guess is as good as anyone else's."

"Hani, you've always impressed me, but tonight, even more so. That you are a master in bao and chess, including Byzantine chess, astonishes me." Mark beamed at his old friend.

Hani laughed the laugh Mark remembered so well. His simple fascination with the world and all things in it was evident in Hani's laughter, giving it a joyful quality that caused Mark and Malcolm to smile broadly at both him and each other.

"But you haven't asked me about Go," Hani reminded them.

Malcolm responded swiftly. "Of course, Hani. I read that in your file. The Chinese friends of your brother-in-law introduced you to Go at an early age also, right?"

"Ten. I was ten years old."

"Mark," Ambassador Wyle explained, trying to compensate for his lack of factual knowledge, "chess is a simulated head-on battle with the objective of total victory or defeat. The aim of Go is relative advantage, to increase your options and reduce those of the adversary. The goal is less about victory and more about persistent strategic progress. It is consistent with the Chinese mentality in this part of the world—I see it demonstrated every day."

Hani elaborated. "Go begins with an empty board and has no limitations. It is simple and elegant, yet it can be so profound. The Chinese have been playing it for 4,000 years. I think it informs their philosophy as much as chess inspires in the West that kind of narrow, rapid, predictable win-lose thinking found in nearly everything." Hani directed himself at Malcolm when he added, "The Chinese are in for the long pull."

Mark looked at Hani, hoping he'd notice that Mark wanted to ask about Mr. Li. His old friend did pick up on it.

"Okay, Malcolm, Mark saw me with Li Jihua that night at the Nairobi Club. He's probably wondering if it's okay to ask about him, since the USA and the Chinese seem to be in some sort of competition out here. Maybe you should respond."

"Sure. Officially, we don't like Mr. Li. Unofficially, I can't say that I do, either, but he personifies the Go mentality we are speaking about. He is everywhere and seems to always know more about things than what we are getting in the message traffic. We need Hani, and Hani seems comfortable with their relationship. Li is likely a spook, but I don't know for whose side. Frankly, I don't trust him at all."

"And that's a good thing," Hani replied. "You diplomats aren't supposed to trust anyone, just report what you know, what you learn, and what you are capable of finding out."

The evening passed too quickly for Mark, but neither he nor Hani wanted to overstay the ambassador's hospitality.

They all presumed they would be meeting again soon, but Jamison was abruptly called back to Washington, DC the following evening. He would have to conclude his work with the commercial and foreign ministries in Muscat and express his gratitude to Sultan Qaboos through his assistants, and there was only time for a quick call to Ambassador Wyle, who promised to explain his hurried departure to Hani Waladoon. Wyle reminded Jamison that he could never speak of Hani's relationship to the ambassador or of their dinner together. It would have to be a very pleasant evening that never took place.

Wyle sent his driver to the al Falaj Hotel to take Jamison to his midnight departure. An aircraft was parked on the tarmac, and Mark was directed to climb aboard through its open door. He whistled a tune as he went up the steps, eager to get back home and having downed a few scotch and waters in preparation for the flight. He was taken aback by what greeted him at the top of the stairway.

The darkened aircraft was full of some of the most miserable looking people he had ever seen. Babies were crying in the arms of hot, sweaty mothers and irate fathers, who were being made to wait in the plane on the ground without air conditioning or air circulation and no permission to leave the plane. One of the women spoke loudly to him.

"So, you're the reason they've held the plane here these past two hours."

"Beats me. Where are you all from?"

"Sydney, on the way to London. Two refueling stops before this one."

"How long have you been on this thing?"

"Seventeen hours, and we still have five to go."

"Gosh." That situation was the modern equivalent to steerage in the old steamship days, only those held in steerage could at least stretch their legs. He slouched down in his seat, happy to be in the first row and by what little breeze was caught by the open door. He willed himself into a lovely sleep that continued until the plane's touchdown at Heathrow.

He spent a comfortable overnight in Knightsbridge, and then it was on to Dulles and an early return to Foggy Bottom and the Department of State. A careful debriefing and the finalizing of agreements prepared in Oman followed. He came back to all the hype of a presidential election, with Jimmy Carter fighting for a second term that was not to be.

The fifty-two American hostages were released on January 20, 1981, 444 days after their kidnapping and 2 months after Mark's return to the United States. Mark's mother was convinced that it resulted from his time in Oman, but he told her it had nothing to do with the hostages. Of course not.

CHAPTER

11

Washington, DC—1983

Two years and several overseas assignments passed by quickly. Work in Main State, or Foggy Bottom, as the State Department was often referred to by insiders, was progressing nicely, and Jamison was delighted to be out for a lunchtime stroll one afternoon. He was determined to finally find out the value of the old silver coins he had purchased in Oman, so he had the list of coins tucked away in his wallet and had checked the phone book for coin dealers that morning. This would be the day to learn how big a fortune his $12.50 weights would yield. He kept the coins themselves in a safety deposit box.

F.C. Gottlieb and Sons, Numismatists, had a basement entrance on M Street NW. He walked down the steps and heard the bell ring inside as he opened the door and pushed his way into the cramped quarters. A middle-aged, somewhat portly gentleman wearing a soiled brown vest and wire-rimmed glassed pulled low on his nose, sporting a pencil mustache underneath it, appeared behind the cluttered counter a moment later. Jamison hoped he hadn't interrupted the man's lunch as he explained the reason for his visit.

"I returned a few years ago from a very remote part of the world with some very old and rare coins. I made a list of them, but I certainly don't expect you to look them up now—"

The fellow snatched the list out of Jamison's hand before he'd finished his sentence and began reading.

"As I was saying," Mark continued, "my phone number is on the list as well, and I would appreciate a call within a few days, if possible, or whenever you can determine their value." Jamison was dealing with the matter as gingerly as if he'd brought back artifacts akin to the Dead Sea Scrolls.

The numismatist looked up and studied him for a few moments before speaking. "They're worth $12.50 each."

"You're kidding. How were you able to know that so quickly?"

"$12.50. You want cash for them?"

"No—I mean, I didn't think you'd be familiar with something this old and rare."

"$12.50, cash. Take it or leave it."

So much for any thought of ignorance in remote places that didn't have telephones, electricity, or newspapers, let alone a hint of any precursor to anything electronic.

Something in the shopkeeper's gaze seemed to assess Mark as thoroughly as any rare coin. Jamison felt compelled to speak up. "You sure seem to know your stuff. May I ask your name?"

"I'm Gottlieb, the owner. Your slip of paper says you're Mark Jamison. Mind if I hang on to this?"

"Not at all. Maybe you can find someone offering a higher figure. Thank you for your help."

Mark turned to leave the shop, but doubled back at the sight of an old, ornate chess set displayed beyond the counter. "You handle chess sets too?"

"On rare occasions, for particular customers."

"Know anything about Byzantine chess?" The words left Jamison's mouth, and he immediately regretted uttering them. Gottlieb resumed his study of Jamison as he slowly shook his head from side to side.

"Don't even know what it is."

Jamison turned and left, thinking nothing more about the encounter until an interesting call came a few days later at the phone number he'd left on the piece of paper entrusted to Gottlieb.

"Mr. Jamison, we haven't met before. My name is Li Jihua. Please call me back."

The number Li left was disconnected, and the telephone company had no record of an account for him or a forwarding number. He thought of calling Gottlieb, but decided to forget it. He was busy with many things and travels in many directions.

Two years later, he received another call from Mr. Li, this time providing no callback number. The message was very brief and troubling:

"Mr. Jamison, we think you have something of ours."

The only thing Jamison could think of was one of his Maria Theresa coins, still in his Riggs Bank safety deposit box, but those coins couldn't be it. Why would Li be interested in common scale weights from Oman that had no connection to him, in any event?

The call from Ambassador Malcolm Wyle came sometime after that, inviting him to lunch at the Cosmos Club. Membership there required an ambassadorship, a flag rank, a full professorship, and the like. At that time, Helen Keller was the only female who had been admitted. Jamison looked forward to invitations to dine there, and catching up with Ambassador Wyle would be great. The ambassador might even have news from Hani or some idea of how to reach him.

It turned out that Wyle was recently retired from government service and wanted to recruit Jamison to join him at his new law partnership with Domich&Carey, a nationwide law firm representing a number of interesting overseas clients including some developing oil pipelines in the Middle East. Wyle spoke of his firm's clients, including the well-known Bechmann Engineering, and of his personal representation of the Xinjiang D'Fray Group, one of the fastest growing new capitalist groups to skirt the laws of the still-very-communist Peoples Republic of China. Wyle wanted to discuss the possibility of Jamison running a newly established overseas office of Domich&Carey.

Jamison listened politely and attentively to Wyle's law firm proposal, but was then focused on his career at the State Department and on a particular young lady named Sarah he was escorting around Washington, DC, so was not interested in a new position. Still, he wanted to learn more of what Domich&Carey was up to and how Wyle came to be representing a client based in the far west of China.

At lunch in a public space, neither felt free to openly discuss Hani Waladoon, though he was clearly on both their minds. Neither ventured to speculate aloud about what matters he was able to assist in resolving with his formidable skills. All each asked was a simple, "Have you heard from him?" to which each responded negatively. Wyle added incongruously, "Well, if you need to reach him, contact me."

They had a few more lunches together, including an interesting one in the Old Ebbitt Grill, very near to the White House.

It seemed that the entire town was abuzz with hushed meetings in corridors and restaurants about the riches to be had from oil and natural gas pipelines. Various proposals were being lobbied hard on Capitol Hill by the M Street powerbrokers like Domich&Carey and their hugely successful client Bechmann Engineering as the big law firms were cashing in on competing pipeline plans. The various routes these pipelines would take would determine which countries would be able to exact transit fees for every barrel passing through their territory. The big winners would be the countries with terminals, enabling them to charge larger fees and providing the leverage to control where the oil would go.

Jamison always liked to arrive early for meetings, but Malcolm Wyle arrived even earlier than Mark for their Old Ebbitt lunch meeting and was engaged in an animated conversation when Mark spotted him at his table. Mark hung back and remained invisible, blending into the crowd at the bar while he observed the small group seated opposite the retired ambassador. As they got up to leave, Jamison was completely taken aback—the face of F.C. Gottlieb emerged among the small group with Wyle. Why would a rare coin dealer know Wyle?

Mark waited a few minutes after the group departed before he approached the table. Wyle quickly slipped a slender file of papers into his case when he glanced up and found Mark approaching.

"Mark, it's so good of you to join me here. The office is just a few blocks away, and I find this place a good spot to get work done and stay visible as one of the players."

"Good to be with you, as always, Malcolm. I never think of you as a player so much as a coach who formulates and calls the shots."

As they were sitting down, Wyle said, "Well, it's thoughtful of you to say that. I like to leave folks with that impression, but Domich&Carey is full of very influential folks. I'm a much smaller fish here than I was out on the Gulf, and the game is a lot bigger, too.

Jamison decided to keep quiet about the unusual company he observed Wyle keeping shortly before. Mark was beginning to get a different sense about Wyle. The once-public servant now considered himself a player, and players in Washington, DC knew few rules. If Wyle was now a player, what was the game?

When the conversation again returned to Mark joining the law firm, Jamison said that his mind was made up. He would be leaving the State Department, but only temporarily, in order to take up a Fulbright teaching fellowship in international law at the University of Salzburg. Wyle congratulated him and reminded him to stay close in coming years.

"If you ever change your mind and want to give private practice a shot, let me know."

"Thanks, Malcolm. I'm sure we'll be running into each other before too long."

They parted company after a cordial lunch together. Jamison still wondered about F.C. Gottlieb, but then it occurred to him that Wyle probably also brought coins back from Oman. This would explain how he might have come to meet Gottlieb and how Gottlieb would have been so familiar with the value of the coins. It was possible that their conversation at that table was even about that. Still, on the walk back to the State Department, Jamison couldn't shake the thought of some connection between Gottlieb and Bechmann or Xinjiang D'Fray, or maybe even both.

PART III

CHAPTER

12

Salzburg, Austria—1989

On his Fulbright professorship in Salzburg in 1983, Mark Jamison was joined by his new bride, Sarah, who shared a modest apartment with a spectacular view of the Untersberg and the Austrian alps with him.

When they returned to Salzburg in 1989 to accept his appointment as the director of the Global Forum, he and Sarah were the happily married parents of two small children, Adam and Adrienne, who fully enjoyed life in a baroque castle with forty acres of grounds and a private lake.

The faculty and fellows who streamed in and out for one-week sessions with the Global Forum were among the world's best and brightest minds. One of the less impressive of these minds belonged a vice rector of the Leningrad State University who had previously received a law degree there in 1975. He was included among the guests the Jamisons hosted in their private quarters the evening before the program's first session. Glasnost and Perestroika in the Soviet Union and liberalizations occurring in Eastern Europe signaled a transformation that occupied that particular week. The vice rector's name was Vladimir Putin.

Putin's German was excellent because, as it turned out, he had just completed a five-year posting in Dresden with the KGB. In fact, while attending the Global Forum as a university vice rector, he also held the rank of lieutenant colonel in the KGB. Jamison smiled upon learning this because he also held a military rank at the same time as his position at the Global Forum, and it was higher than Putin's.

Neither showed particular interest in the other at the time. Viktor Churkin, the head of the Soviet Academy of Sciences and a long-time supporter of the Forum, held Jamison's attention in matters Russian. A university vice rector struck Jamison as a less than dynamic, engaging figure. Still, Putin and Jamison exchanged greetings in German and English and occasionally a few words in Russian while engaged in break-out sessions or preparing faxes in the castle's baroque library, above its marble hall. Jamison didn't realize then that he would soon be joining Putin in sending messages to the same figure in the Vatican—Cardinal Ratzinger.

Putin realized that the end of the Soviet Union was rapidly approaching. The Russia that would emerge—and he, personally—would require important friends and support from outside the country, friends like those controlling the intelligence service of the Vatican and maybe even those involved with the Global Forum. In their brief exchanges, Putin occasionally asserted that the Orthodox Church was the true successor to the Church of Peter and that Russia would be its natural protector.

Putin had historical support for his claims. In 800, the authority of the Roman Empire was located in Byzantium and the Eastern Church was headquartered in the Cathedral of the Hagia Sophia, the Holy Wisdom of God, which had been constructed in 530. In the eyes of many, although converted to a mosque, it remains today the most spiritually beautiful church ever built.

Between 800 and 1100, the Byzantine Empire developed a relationship with the new state of Kievan Rus, which emerged to the north and across the Black Sea. After initial military encounters, the Empire used religion to achieve its aims toward Kievan Rus through a royal marriage and the Christianization of the Rus in 988. Byzantine clergy, architects, and artists went to work on what would become Russia's most celebrated cathedrals and churches.

In stark contrast, the competing bishops of Rome and the papacy that remained in what would become Italy was riven with illegitimacy, including the unilateral declaration in 800 by Pope Leo III that Frankish King Charlemagne would be the successor to the Western emperors in what would become the Holy Roman Empire, which is remembered for being neither holy or Roman, nor an empire at all. The developing reality was the commercial competition between the old center of trade and power in Constantinople and the growing power and commercial interests of Genoa and Venice in the West. Constantinople was seen to be holding this Western growth in check.

The schism between the Western and Eastern Churches occurred on July 16, 1054. Three papal legates from Rome entered the Hagia Sophia during the Divine Liturgy and placed a bull of excommunication on the altar. Though calls for unity of the two Churches went out many times thereafter, they were never heeded by the West.

With the conquest of Byzantium by the Turks in 1453, the role of emperor in the East was claimed by Ivan III, whose grandson would be the first tsar of Russia. The term "tsar" originates from the Latin *Caesar*, which the Slavs traditionally called the Byzantine emperors. Interestingly, the conquering Muslim Sultan Mehmed II also claimed the title of Kaysari Rum and regarded himself as an "heir" of Byzantium and Rome.

Putin began including aspects of his knowledge of the subject into his reports to the Vatican along with news of the financial meltdown occurring within the Soviet system and other newsworthy items.

To his surprise, the Vatican replied with an obvious interest in his historical narrative. In particular, they were interested in what he knew or could learn about the whereabouts of the Byzantine *Liberia* following the Turkish conquest. Had the vast historical archives and treasures been destroyed, captured by the Turks, or transferred out of Constantinople before the attack? Did Ivan the Terrible take them northward and hide them within Russia? They were interested in the answers to these questions.

The Vatican was aware that claims of representing the Third Rome had been kept alive by the Russian royals and Orthodox patriarchs until the murder of the final tsar, Nicholas II, during the Bolshevik Revolution. If the Orthodox Church could be revived following the Soviet collapse, would Moscow seek once again to claim to be the protector of the Faithful?

It seemed that Putin kept the dialogue on this subject alive just to see where it might go, even intimating that he had seen evidence suggesting the *Liberia* had been hidden in tunnels deep under the Kremlin, long ago lost and forgotten. He also had other thoughts on the subject.

While discussing the matter with historians at Leningrad State University once, he was reminded that the Hagia Sophia was considerably older than Russian Christianity; when Constantine moved from Rome to Byzantium, much of Anatolia was already Christian. The first Christian nation was Armenia, they told him, and its Cathedral of Echzmiatzin, still in use today, was erected in 301 AD. The Armenians were Christian while Rome remained pagan and long before Russia ever existed.

It was just possible, the historians informed him, that in the final years before the conquest, Byzantine treasures could have found their way to the Armenians still holding out from the Turks in Cilicia and engaged in vigorous commercial dealings with Venice. If this was the case, it would have been a simple matter to take these archives and treasures from Armenian Cilica, on the southern coast of Anatolia, to Venice on Armenian commercial ships, flotillas of which departed regularly from Ayas—and also from today's Izmir, near to Constantinople—bound for Venice. These academics even suggested the likelihood of this being arranged by Venice's Doge Sebastiano when he lived in Cilician Armenia as ambassador of the Serene Republic in 1253.

Knowledge of these rumors may have explained why the vice rector from Leningrad State University asked Mark Jamison if it was true that his mother was Armenian in one of their short exchanges.

"How would you know that, Vladimir?"

"Well, Russia always thinks about its friends, wherever they are located, and we think a lot of the Armenians, in general. Ever been to San Lazaro?"

"Why do you ask?"

Each immediately suspected that the other was not what he outwardly seemed, so the subject was quickly changed to the content of the Forum's plenary session planned for the following morning.

Jamison thought nothing more about his guest or this exchange until after the conclusion of that group of sessions. His young son helped with the reception and farewell parties taking place in the Jamisons' private quarters in the castle. Dressed in a blue blazer and necktie, six-year-old Adam would take the guests' coats and help arrange drink orders with the staff—always aided by his younger sister, Adrienne, of course—and guests from the East would frequently gift him with coins for his efforts.

A few days following the session involving Putin, Jamison found Adam playing with some coins on his bed. One large gold coin caught Mark's attention. Picking it up, he saw the figure of a Byzantine emperor playing chess. Looking closer, he saw that the board was circular. The other side depicted an early Roman Catholic pope.

"Adam, where did you get this? Who gave it to you?"

His answer was very clear and immediate: "Pootin."

"Did he say anything when he gave it to you?"

"He said, 'Good boy.'"

Putin had to know that Jamison would see the coin. It was recently minted and contained no date or details, just the message in its depictions. Was it meant to be a reproduction of a real coin or just a message that Mr. Putin was sending Mark about a parallel interest?

CHAPTER

13

Salzburg was a wonderful venue from which to witness the unraveling of the Soviet Union and the Warsaw Pact. A stream of newly visa-eligible Hungarians poured into Austria, and then when East Germans realized they were allowed to go to Hungary, the procession of little Trabant automobiles comprised a flood of families escaping westward from East Germany through Hungary and then across the border to Austria and the freedom of the West.

The rallies that resulted in the new freedoms in Eastern Europe and the eventual collapse of the Soviet Union were all held after working hours. It was inconceivable to most people that the monolith of the Soviet Union could crumble without bloodshed or, since the rallies were held in the evenings, so much as an hour of missed work. Only in Romania did the old guard attempt to fight, and the roundup of the fleeing dictator Nicolae Ceausescu and his wife Elena provided spectacular news footage. Jamison, later dubbed the "oracle" for his ability to forecast these coming events, had predicted that the Berlin Wall would come down, but no one, including Jamison, could predict that the entire edifice of the Soviet Union would disintegrate.

Maybe it began when a teenage youth from West Germany named Mathias Rust took off in a single-engine private airplane and flew across East Germany and into Russia, landing in Red Square. The entire Soviet air defense system was at once shown to be as hollow and ridiculous as the whole of the state security apparatus. Suddenly, the Soviet bear appeared as naked as a wild bear in the woods. This image was certainly also fueled by the developing revelations of Gorbachev's Glasnost and Perestroika. People simply stopped being afraid of a system that no longer worked, and hadn't worked in a very long time.

The inevitable reaction was fully anticipated, though. A group of old-school hardliners appeared on television announcing that they were taking charge of the country and replacing Gorbachev, who had been placed in house arrest, but even they didn't look like they should have been taken seriously. They looked like they were put up to it, like they didn't really want to bother with running the bankrupt mess that was the Soviet administration.

Things went silent for a time after this. Those hardliners just disappeared, and matters became fluid. Tanks approached Moscow, and its daring mayor, Boris Yeltsin, said there was no going back. It was like the Wild West as a high drama played out, televised in astonishing clarity. There was a public meeting chaired by a standing Yeltsin who improvised his way along, shouting for any lawyer present to verbally fill in any legal gaps in the proceedings.

The mystery of the disappearance of the hardliners and its aftermath led to speculation about some decision-making process that was fast, arbitrary, effective, and bloodless, and that all involved parties had agreed to this process in advance. The rumor spread of one or more board games determining the outcome and that a shadowy figure called the Game Master was actually the one responsible for the tanks stopping their firing after a late-night session involving three chess champions. No one could confirm or deny the reports, but everyone relaxed in apparent satisfaction that no further confrontations would be mounted in Russia and East Europe.

The situation in Russia was reflected also in disputes that were arising in the newly independent republics, especially in areas previously carved up by Stalin in an effort to keep Moscow as the essential element in achieving peace and stability.

Reports began coming into Mark Jamison's office at the Global Forum in Salzburg pertaining to Armenia. He received word that the massacres of ethnic Armenians by Azeri Turks in Sumgait, Baku and other parts of Azerbaijan that had begun the year before were turning increasingly violent and widespread. The report stated that part of the ancient Armenian homeland, a mountainous region called Nagorno Karabagh, was an autonomous oblast that had been pulled from Armenia's administration and cynically placed under Azerbaijan's by Stalin in the 1920s. When the Soviet Union broke apart, the autonomous region petitioned to be administered by Armenia, and the reaction of Azerbaijanis was mass looting and killing of Armenians being carried out even while Turkey continued to deny the Genocide and jailed those who openly discussed the issue. At every turn, Turkey was supporting its Turkic cousins in Azerbaijan; they even instituted a total blockade of land-locked Armenia, which wasn't a party to the issue.

Mark feared a war was coming that would continue the old pan-Turkic plan at the time of the Genocide in order to link Turkey with the oilfields of Baku. As before in Nagorno Karabagh, only the Armenians stood in the way. It looked as if the effort at total eradication would be once again under-way in earnest. As he watched with growing trepidation, the enclave of Karabagh was besieged by the vastly superior army of oil-rich Azerbaijan.

News also reached Jamison about the fact that Armenia's and Azerbaijan's chess champions were standing near the very pinnacle of world titles. If the shadowy figure he continued to hear about, the Game Master, was indeed his old friend Hani Waladoon, maybe it was time to contact him and get him involved in a peaceful resolution of this bloody confrontation. Mark reached out to former-Ambassador Wyle. Sure enough, Malcolm Wyle knew how to reach Hani.

CHAPTER

14

Letter from Mark Jamison to Hani Waladoon, April 24, 1990

My dear Hani,

I write to you only to give some background to what you must already be reading about in the media. You certainly recall that members of my mother's family were Armenian Genocide survivors, and I can't bear to see a continuation of the slaughter, even while the genocide itself was never acknowledged by the perpetrators. Hani, if you can help, please do your best. Please excuse my presumption at informing you on the issue, because you are probably better informed than I am, but your old friend is upset and wants to share this with you.

We both know that the Turks have been on the wrong side of history since 1515, when they banned the publication of books within the extensive Ottoman Empire. Not surprisingly, the empire didn't stay extensive for long, as Western astonishment at the incredible cruelty of the Turks toward the indigenous Christian populations led to support for rebellions in Greece, the Balkans, and elsewhere.

It was a different story, however, for Christian minorities in other Ottoman regions. While the Orthodox Russian tsars sought repeatedly to come to their aid, the British feared Russian territorial encroachments more than they were concerned with the dreadful condition of the minority populations in these regions. England propped up the ailing "Sick Man of Europe," as the Ottoman Empire was then known, in exchange for naval bases on Cyprus and other gifts given by the Turks to induce the British to turn a blind eye toward the deprivation, torture, and murder without legal recourse of their fellow Christians. The height of official British indifference to these humanitarian concerns of course came when they joined with the Turks in the mid-nineteenth century to go to war with Russia to keep it out of that region in the intensely unpopular Crimean War.

Despite the cold calculations of its strategy makers, the British Parliament continued to be aghast at the torture and massacres that the Turks seemed to relish inflicting on defenseless Christians at every opportunity. Following the misadventure that was the war, the British and other Western powers began demanding Turkish reforms and some semblance of justice for the innocents trapped within the oppressive dominion of the Sublime Porte. There ensued a cat-and-mouse game of mass murder and concealment by the Turks from Western observers, which extended through the remaining life of the "Sick Man of Europe"—until the first world war.

The Turks again chose the wrong side of history in that conflict by joining with the Germans against the allied powers. They used the pretext of that war to commit a mass murder so large in scale that it required a new term to characterize it: Genocide, the extermination of an entire race of people. This honor fell, of course, to the unfortunate Armenians, descendants of a once-mighty imperial power that had occupied much of Anatolia for thousands of years and which had become the first Christian nation many hundreds of years before the arrival of the Ottoman Turks and their overwhelming martial prowess.

It was during the period of cosmetic reforms and independence movements encouraged by the West before the first world war, and due in large part to the education provided mainly by American Protestant missionaries, that the Armenians decided to explore expanding their rights from a status equated to that of cattle and pigs to a status more in line with that of their "human" Muslim overlords.

Their first meetings with the Ottoman authorities in 1895 to broach the subject resulted in the mass killing of over 300,000 Armenians for showing such impertinence. During World War I, that number paled to relative insignificance as the modern, reformed Turkish state undertook the total annihilation of the population, now most accurately described as nearly two million souls.

The even more modern Turkish Republic that emerged after the war continued the same policy of killing and destruction of Armenians with simultaneous denial. Kemal Attaturk led his forces eastward to finish off the few emaciated survivors who had gathered on historic lands to the east of Turkey. This ragtag army of volunteers nearly succumbed, which would have led to the utter destruction of the entire people, but they held the line at Sardarabad. They were then swallowed by the Russians into the new Soviet gulag as the Armenian Soviet Socialist Republic. Some of the historic Armenian lands and populations were even further carved up by Stalin and given over to the administration of Azerbaijan. This move was designed to keep Moscow in the center of relations in the Caucasus. This revealed Stalin's characteristic cruelty, because it was and is a known fact that Azeris were and remain a Muslim Turkic people who identified with those who had taken the vast majority of Armenian lands and killed off nearly the entire population in the past.

While modern Turkey continued to destroy Armenian churches and worked quietly to obliterate any traces of Armenia's cultural legacy, the West continued to turn a blind eye because of growing economic interests. That the world let Turkey get away with one of the greatest crimes in all history was not without global consequences, though. In fact, when questioned by some of his generals about how he thought he could get away with his planned extermination of European Jewry, Hitler answered famously, "Who today remembers the Armenians?" After the second world war and in the preoccupation with the Cold War, Turkey became an early member of NATO and the site of valuable US air bases and listening posts on its border with the Soviet Union. The ice-cold calculations and brutal self-interest of British strategists in the nineteenth century were being continued by the Western powers throughout the twentieth century.

The next scent of reform and independence for the Armenians began wafting from Gorbachev's policies of Glasnost and Perestroika when the Armenian enclave of Nagorno Karabagh within Azerbaijan petitioned Moscow to be governed by Yerevan, not Baku, as I mentioned before. As independence came to the Soviet republics, this region sought autonomy. In line with prior experience at the hands of the Turks, this peaceful democratic effort was met with violent pogroms and the destruction of the Armenian communities in Baku and Sumgait without a semblance of Azeri police or other official protection for the Armenians from mob attacks. When autonomy was not achieved, Karabagh voted for independence from Azerbaijan, which responded by attacking the enclave with its considerable army. This time, unlike the Armenian Genocide seventy-five years earlier, the Armenians fought back effectively and maintained their independence, though it remains secured only by a tenuous cease fire even today. Azeri snipers continually violate its terms, and an airport built in Nagorno Karabagh has yet to receive an aircraft because of Azeri threats to shoot it down. When an Azeri beheaded a sleeping Armenian officer during a NATO training session in Budapest, he returned to a hero's welcome in Azerbaijan, whose foreign minister declared Armenians everywhere enemies of his country.

For its part, Turkey immediately assisted Azerbaijan during this conflict by blockading its landlocked neighbor, a finally reemerged independent Armenia that was struggling to survive following the economic collapse and breakup of the Soviet Union. The blockade kept heating fuel and food from reaching Armenia, which resulted in more suffering and deaths from Turkey's continuing hostility. Its policies of denial and obliteration of everything associated with historical Armenia continue today as Turkey struggles to erase all references to the victim population and continues persecution and even the occasional murder of those who dare to speak out about the past or to call attention to continuing misdeeds. Turkish scholars who dare to question the record of atrocities are still imprisoned by modern Turkey.

Of course, things are never simple in the Caucasus, where Byzantine mentalities layer over religious, tribal, and family survival skills, resulting in a complexity few outsiders can readily fathom. Stalin's original plan to keep Moscow's control of the region continues to play out in the Nagorno Karabagh stand-off. When the Soviet Union collapsed, Russia called for the creation of the Commonwealth of Independent States, what it termed its near-abroad policy of keeping the newly emerged republics closely tied to Moscow, *but most independent republics were eager to shed their past and thus replaced the old communist bosses, loyal to Moscow, with new independent leaders. Azerbaijan was no exception—it refused to join the Commonwealth. Armenia, still surrounded by hostile Muslim neighbors, readily acceded.*

There are many theories about why Azerbaijan went to war with Nagorno Karabagh, but many blame Russia. Russia may have seen the region's bid for autonomy as an opening to get back into a controlling position in oil-rich Azerbaijan. First, it quietly fanned the flames of anti-Armenian sentiment in Baku and Sumgait, and then it equipped the Azeri army with the means to crush the breakaway enclave. Once the conflict got underway in earnest, it exacted the price of bringing back the old Communist party boss in Azerbaijan and forcing the country to join the Commonwealth for its continued help. Once this deal was secured, Russia provided clandestine support to Karabagh so that it wouldn't lose the conflict. This perpetual regional tension and garnered reliance by both sides on Moscow was straight out of the Stalin playbook. Today, Russia is part of the small group of nations that is seeking to bring about a resolution to this conflict. Of course, it doesn't want victory on either side, but a simmering state of hostilities that will likely continue for the foreseeable future.

The only hope for a real peace is for both sides to construct their own resolution without outside manipulation. Too bad they don't turn the conundrum over to their best brain trusts—the chess masters both sides boast are among the greatest in the world. Then, you probably already know that and everything else I just communicated to you. I suppose I am writing this letter to you today because this is the day Armenians around the world commemorate the Armenian Genocide and honor their fallen martyrs.

CHAPTER

15

Vienna

As he concluded the letter to Hani Waladoon, Jamison knew he had to do whatever he could to enlist support for the beleaguered Armenians of Karabagh, and finding arrows for Hani's quiver was one thing he could pursue. If the time ever came for Hani to negotiate a resolution, he wanted his friend to have every advantage, even if it meant scouring the world to find any historical knowledge that might be locked away. Preventing the final end of the ancient race of Armenians would certainly qualify as a good reason to obtain new knowledge.

Jamison recalled an introduction he'd received before leaving the United States for Salzburg to Archbishop Krikor Atemian of Vienna's Saint Hripsime Armenian Apostolic Church. The Armenian Church distinguished itself from other orthodox churches by referring to its founding as directly by apostles. A phone call to Atemian found him very receptive and willing to do whatever he could to help. Atemian mentioned his birthplace was near Stepanakert in Karabagh and that he still had relatives there, so he shared Mark's deep concern for the fighting that was taking place in the region. Atemian said he had cousins hiding in their basements while Azeri shells and rockets attacked them on a daily basis.

Archbishop Atemian invited Mark to take the train to Vienna the following week and promised that he would see what meetings he could arrange. The archbishop told Mark that his first call would be to the Armenian Catholic Prelate in Vienna.

Armenian history in Austria goes back to Vienna's liberation from the Turkish siege. Every Viennese knows that the one benefit of the long siege at its walls was the aroma of Arabica coffee wafting from the Turkish encampment, and the first documented Viennese coffee house was opened in 1685 by an Armenian. In 1775, Empress Maria Theresa gave permission to the Mekhitarist congregation of the Armenian Catholic Church to establish itself in Vienna. It quickly established a publishing and educational center there, along with a repository of manuscripts that was estimated at 153,000 volumes. Its holdings were soon discovered to include ancient artifacts and coins going back to centuries before the birth of Christ.

The prelate told Atemian that he had just the right connection for Mark Jamison. He would arrange for him to meet with the dynamic, young Roman Catholic archbishop at St. Stephens who was very knowledgeable about the Eastern Christians and connected at the highest levels at the Vatican. He had been a graduate student at Tubingen and had later served on its faculty. The prelate had already held discussions with him about the enormous destruction of Christian populations in the Middle East and the apparent determination of Turkey to finish what it started earlier in the century in relation to Armenians. This archbishop's name was Juergen Scheuer.

When Atemian informed Mark of the meeting, he suggested the two of them first get together to discuss the best approach in regard to the Catholic archbishop, so Jamison met with Atemian at St. Hripsme the day before his scheduled meeting with Scheuer.

"The Roman Catholics will want something. They can be of enormous good to us, but they never have stood up for the Eastern Christians before. Never. You must be a real diplomat in this endeavor, Mark. You will have to get his attention and then the Vatican's.

"The prelate helped me do some research on Scheuer: He is very close to Cardinal Ratzinger, who runs the Vatican for Pope John Paul II. Ratzinger is the keeper of doctrine, but he also runs their intelligence network and their archives. He and Scheuer are as good a pair as we will ever find to help us, but you'll have to capture their interest with more than the obvious humanitarian concerns."

"I certainly see your point and will do my best, but what do you suggest?"

"Ratzinger obviously loves secrets. He probably knows more of them than you or I could even imagine. People like him always want to know everything.

"Scheuer is very interested in what the Mekhitarists hold in their archives. The prelate really got his attention when he told him they have only a small fraction of what the orthodox Mother Church keeps safe to itself. You can play on this. I don't know exactly what secrets will appeal to them, but you have to intrigue their interest and hold it. The Vatican wants to know everything, and we in the Eastern Church have never been open with it, just as it hasn't been with us.

"Be careful when you meet with Scheuer—he is a chess player. They all are. Ratzinger is probably a master chess player. The Vatican insiders thrive on it."

"I think you have just given me what I need."

"I hope so, Mark. Can we meet again after you finish your meeting with Scheuer?"

"Of course."

"Let's meet at Café Central the next time. I like to get out of here and enjoy good coffee. Do you know the place? It's not far from Stephansdom. Phone me when you conclude the meeting and walk over there."

The following morning, Mark walked from his hotel across Stephans Platz and met with Archbishop Scheuer. Scheuer began the conversation by talking about his fascination with the Armenians. He informed Mark of recent archeological discoveries, which included a pair of perfectly made and preserved leather shoes, complete with laces, that were found to be 5,500 years old. Nearby in Armenia was a complete, sophisticated winery that confounded everyone when it was carbon tested and found to be 6,100 years old.

"So why wouldn't Armenia be the oldest Christian nation, when it now appears to be the oldest nation?" Scheuer finished. "They are a people that refuse to die."

Mark took the cue and suggested that there were those still adamantly trying to destroy them and informing the archbishop of that situation. Scheuer listened intently and said he fully shared Jamison's concerns. The archbishop showed himself much better informed than Mark ever imagined, and his quick mind and enormous reservoir of knowledge dazzled Jamison.

"You know that Lord Byron lived many months with the Mekhitarists at San Lazaro," Scheuer went on to inform Mark. "He learned the Armenian language and even wrote books in Armenian. He wanted to replace the Biblical story of Cain with that of Haik, the great-great grandson of Noah who became the founding patriarch of the Armenians."

If Mark's mouth wasn't agape, he wondered why he felt he should close it.

Scheuer continued. "Lord Byron wrote in his memoirs that 'God speaks to the world in Armenian.' He was that impressed with the elegant simplicity of the language and what he discovered there."

Again, Jamison took the cue to proceed. "And it may be that secrets were shared with him there—secrets that Lord Byron took to his grave at Missologni, fighting the Turks."

Scheuer leaned forward slightly. "And what secrets would those be, Mark?"

Jamison quickly thought back to what Atemian had said about hooking Scheuer's interest and what he'd learned of chess variants from Hani in Oman.

"Well, of course, the secrets of Lord Byron remain secret, but I have heard a little about some knowledge that goes back to the Byzantine days, and maybe even earlier. Have you heard of Byzantine chess?"

The relationship had begun. Jamison and Scheuer had hooked each other. At the end of two hours of intense conversation, Mark agreed to share information with Jeurgen Scheuer, who agreed to pass it along to the Vatican. Scheuer promised to be as helpful as he could when it came to intervening to save their fellow Christians in peril in the East.

Jamison left St. Stephen's Cathedral that morning feeling like it had been the most important morning of his life. In that short time, he may have built a solid relationship with a controlling power of one of the most controlling powers the world has ever known. He telephoned Archbishop Atemian and headed for the Café Central.

As he walked across the huge square, the weight of serious realization pressed in on him. He would now need to find out a great deal more of the secrets of the Byzantine Empire. Many lives might actually depend on it.

Mark arrived first and took a table, greeting Atemian when he entered and sat down. "So, Archbishop Atemian, are you by any chance a chess player?"

"Why yes, certainly I play—not very well, I'm afraid, but I do play. I am Armenian, after all. Why do you ask?"

"Do you happen to know any secret history of the game? Anything that may have been safeguarded over the years? Anything relating to Byzantine chess, maybe?"

"I take it you tried whetting Archbishop's Scheuer's appetite with this. How did he react?"

"I used that, yes…And this." Mark pulled a small purple pouch from his pocket and extracted the gold coin that Putin gave to his son.

Archbishop Atemian studied the coin, appearing excited by it.

"Where in the world did you get this?" Without waiting for an answer, he continued. "Scheuer will no doubt be sharing everything about this with Cardinal Ratzinger."

"One of the participants at a Global Forum seminar gave it to my son—a Russian academic."

"Mark, I think you will find that there are some secrets still about the game. I recall hearing something about this initially when I was in seminary and again at a council of bishops meeting at Echmiadzin. How did you find Scheuer?"

"I think he's brilliant."

"That's what I've heard. Will he help us?"

"I think it will take a while, and we'll have to build up more trust with him, but he might."

"Mark, I have been giving a lot of thought to all this. If you are serious about finding out about our past in order to help our people, I think you must pay a visit to the Patriarch in Jerusalem. He knows a great deal and can unlock many doors. After all, everything is a secret until you discover it for yourself…And be sure you show him that coin.

"In the meanwhile, please be extremely discrete. The Church holds secrets and must carefully safeguard them. It is both how we have survived and how we will continue surviving. I wish you much success in anything you endeavor to do for our people. Will you go to Jerusalem after this?"

"I have responsibilities awaiting me in Salzburg and have a class starting up next week in London."

"Are they truly more important than this?" Atemian clutched Mark's arm and whispered to him, "I think you should go directly from here, as soon as possible. Things are not right in Jerusalem, and you could be helpful to the Patriarch. I will phone him and have your visas available in the morning."

Mark hesitated.

"Yes. You'll go straight away?"

Two sighs later, Jamison shrugged his shoulders.

"I'll call Salzburg from my hotel and see about arranging things," he promised Atemian. "Sarah is there with the children. Thank you, Father."

They both stood up to go, and Mark bent over to kiss the archbishop's ring in the ancient Orthodox tradition. Atemian pushed him back.

"We are modern here, Mark. Now be on your way and may God grant you safe passage."

CHAPTER

16

Jerusalem

Jamison was met at Ben Gurion International Airport by a sign-carrying young man named Bedros who introduced himself as the assistant to the Patriarch's secretary. Bedros helped Mark with arrival formalities, exchanged some currency for him, and led him outside for a walk of several blocks to a parked old Plymouth.

"This is our transportation. Come on, you're in for a treat." Bedros's sarcasm couldn't be missed. He threw open the passenger door, and Mark got into a seat without discernible support or seat belts. It was like arriving in Cuba.

"Hope you weren't expecting a limousine," the assistant added while gunning the engine. "Don't worry, it will get us there." In a cloud of black smoke, the car lunged forward and into the bristling traffic headed for Jerusalem and the Old City.

It had been more than twenty years since Mark was last here, and he enjoyed the ride while holding onto anything he could to keep his balance.

"What do you have against seat belts?"

"We tend to pray a lot around here," Bedros responded, throwing the car into a sudden lane change without signaling. "They're here somewhere. It's the law. Would you like a cigarette?" Bedros stared at him when he spoke.

"No, thank you. Shouldn't you keep your eyes on the traffic?"

"Sure, but don't worry. Everyone drives like this around here. Welcome back to the Middle East. I heard you used to live in Lebanon—beautiful up there, with the mountains. We have a few hills here that local folks call mountains. They have never seen Lebanon."

"Do you know where I'll be staying?"

"You'll be in a guest apartment in our quarter. When we get there, I'll take you there first so you can clean up and relax before I walk you over to meet the Patriarch. Whatever you do, remember that the heavy doors are closed and locked at 10 pm, and you must be inside by then. Everyone must be. It is not safe to be outside at night."

"How many is everyone?"

"There are about 2,000 families living in the quarter. No one is very happy with how hard it is to keep things in repair. We need permits for everything and frequently don't get them. We're tolerated here, but there's no question that they want us out. We've never been welcome here.

"Sorry to hear that."

Bedros made another swerve to avoid a lorry that had pulled immediately in front of the surging Plymouth without so much as a glance in the side mirrors first.

"It's nothing we're not used to. There used to be 25,000 families in the quarter, but most have left. The Armenians have been here the longest, though, and will be here long after everyone else."

Bedros swerved to get around the lorry, giving the old V-8 engine every bit of gas his heavy foot could provide.

"Where did you learn such great English?" Mark inquired.

"I'm from New Jersey."

"What brought you here?"

"Der Manoushian. I remember him from New York. I know that his Beatitude is how we *should* refer to him, but I just call him Surpazan Hayr, which is what we call all bishops in Armenian. You can call him that, too. He is probably the finest man walking in this world, and one of the smartest. Guess I'm here just to be near him and do what I can. We've got our hands full here—probably always have."

The Armenian Patriarchate in Jerusalem occupies most of that revered city's Armenian Quarter and has done so since the time of Jesus Christ, if not longer. In fact, some accounts report that Armenian King Tigranes II held Jerusalem for a brief period before being dislodged by the Romans prior to the birth of Christ. There were about seventy Armenian monasteries in the Holy Land, though few of them still had their doors open. The majority had been singled out for demolition or left to decay. Jerusalem's Brotherhood of Saint James monastic community was the home of Patriarch Archbishop Manoug der Manoushian and, for a few days at least, apparently also the new home of Mark Jamison.

"Have you toured the Holy Sepulchre?" Bedros asked as they arrived and passed through security at the gates.

"Many years ago, but I'd love to see it again."

"Let me walk you through before we go to meet the Patriarch. The ladies have prepared some food and left it in your apartment, so get a bite, rest up for an hour, and then I will be by for you. Your meeting is scheduled for four o'clock."

"Thank you, Bedros, I look forward to it. Your driving was great, by the way. What did you do in New Jersey?"

"I drove a taxi while I was in school."

"Should have guessed."

Jamison enjoyed his tour of the Holy Sepulchre an hour later. Inseparable from the Armenian Quarter, the Holy Sepulchre is protected by the Eastern Orthodox, Roman Catholic, and Armenian Apostolic Churches, each of which perform the Divine Liturgy there daily. It encompasses Golgotha, where Jesus of Nazareth was crucified, as well as the place of his entombment and resurrection. Construction of the church was begun in 325 AD, shortly after

Christianity was permitted as a religion by Rome in 313. Byzantine Emperor Constantine's mother, Helena, was the inspiration for the church. Construction began following her visit to the Holy Land and rediscovery of the true Cross.

Meeting the Patriarch at four o'clock was an astonishing experience for Jamison. He remembered Mark from earlier meetings in San Francisco, which took place more than thirty years before when der Manoushian was a young bishop based in Los Angeles with responsibility for the Western US. It was more than Mark could have hoped for, and it was clearly a sign that the Patriarch's administrative and organizational skills were extraordinary.

Dressed in a simple black cassock adorned with a jeweled silver cross pendant for their meeting, der Manushian remained a strikingly handsome man, even with the creases now evident in his face and the white hair that capped his still-athletic six foot frame. They talked first about family and friends in common from the early days and then about Jamison's visit with Archbishop Atemian in Vienna.

"Mark, I understand that you have been asking about chess—Byzantine chess, to be exact. It is how we have survived for more than 4,000 years as a people. We play chess here every day to survive. I am sitting atop a lineage of Armenian patriarchs in Jerusalem that goes back to 638. Can you imagine that? This is the most volatile and coveted land in the entire world, and we have held this ground through occupations by Byzantines, Persians, Arabs, Crusaders, Turks, the British, and now the Israelis. We get along with everyone and ask only that our places of worship be respected. It was never easy. Nearly all occupiers want complete control over every inch of this ground, and, frankly, most would just as soon be rid of all Christians in the Holy Land. The Middle East used to be the center of the Christian world. Today, most Christians continue to flee this land for their lives and safety."

"I understand," Mark said quietly.

"As you can imagine, we know something about listening carefully and anticipating several moves ahead. Did you know that when the Romans forced the Jews out of Jerusalem in the year 70 AD, the year they call the destruction of Jerusalem, the Romans imported Armenian administrators, architects, builders, and artisans? We were considered loyal Roman subjects. We learned Christianity firsthand while we were here. Around the same time, the apostles Thaddeus and Bartholomew went to Armenia and spread the message of our Lord. Did you know that Thaddeus was our first Catholicos and Bartholomew our second? That's why we call our church Apostolic. We had Eastern Christian pilgrims coming here to the holy sites even during Roman times. While Rome was throwing its Christians to the lions in the Coliseum for entertainment, we had pilgrims coming to the Holy Land to worship secretly in the care of other Armenians. It is no wonder that Armenia became the first nation in the world to declare its Christianity."

"Or that some sense of discomfort might exist here with the Israelis. I mean, if the Romans threw out the Jews and brought in the Armenians in 70 AD, surely that couldn't have rested very well."

"Nothing rests well here with anybody. It is the land of win-lose or, more often, of lose-lose. My Israeli friends tell the story of the frog and scorpion: The scorpion wants to cross the river and asks the frog for a ride across on its back. The frog objects and says, 'You are a scorpion. If I let you on my back, you'll sting me and I will die.' The scorpion reminds the frog that it needs to cross the river and would therefore not harm its conveyance. Finally, the frog relents and they depart. Halfway across the river, the scorpion stings the frog. While they are both drowning, the frog asks the scorpion why it stung him, even knowing they would both die. The scorpion responds, 'Because it is the Middle East,' as they both slip under to their deaths."

Mark smiled, but couldn't muster a laugh. One was not expected.

"Archbishop Atemian suggested you knew more than he about the lost knowledge of the Byzantines, especially about their game of chess." Mark changed the subject. "Perhaps some aspect that was kept secret and hidden away in Byzantine vaults for some special occasion when winning the game could mean the life or death of its culture and people?"

"What do *you* think, Mark? We have the Gulbenkian Library here in the Quarter, but there are no secrets here. This place has never been secure. Where do you think this lost knowledge is hidden?"

Mark was happy to offer up what he knew. "Well, my research would suggest that Armenia was a major center of learning in antiquity and a crossroads of knowledge passing from East to West and South to North. By that, I mean knowledge passing between China, Persia, and India, as well as Greece and Egypt. It would have had treasures written in Greek before its own written language was invented in 405 AD."

"Well done, Mark. And the Byzantines? What do you know of them?"

"The Byzantines took all the knowledge they possessed from ancient Rome and the Roman Empire with them to Constantinople, which fell to the Turks in 1453. While in Byzantium before the fall of Constantinople, the Eastern Romans gathered up all the ancient Greek learning and treasures they could find, just as the Armenians did. Between them, they held incredible stores of knowledge; both groups needed to safeguard it from the marauders of the day. Of course, neither trusted the other, but both knew that all would be lost to the Turks if they didn't remove their treasures to a safe location."

"Again, excellent research, Mark."

"That is where my knowledge becomes less concrete, so please develop this for me further, Surpazan Hayr. The history of Armenia is intertwined with that of the Crusades and of the Holy Land—I know that much."

"Well, I'll do my best. The Byzantines annexed Armenia in 1045. Shortly thereafter, the Seljuk Turks began their conquest of our traditional homeland in Eastern Anatolia, and the Byzantines encouraged the Armenians to move south to Cilicia and establish a defensive line there against the Turks that would also protect the Byzantines. In 1080, Armenian Cilicia was established along the southern coast of Anatolia and running to the Taurus Mountains. Historic Armenia was positioned on the Silk Road; after the establishment of Cilicia, Armenia was positioned on both the Silk Road and the sea lanes to Europe—her commerce flourished. Armenian fleets based in Ayas and other ports carried considerable cargoes across the Mediterranean.

"The new European centers of commerce and industry were Genoa and Venice, which quickly became rivals to Byzantium. The Byzantines locked up traders from these centers when they wouldn't kowtow sufficiently to the emperor and his many restrictive conditions on trade. He ran the empire as if he could control its furthest reaches, but the West was breaking away, so Europe turned to the Armenians in Cilicia. Cilicia grew and expanded, obtaining significant wealth and military power. By 1198, it was elevated from a principality to a recognized kingdom.

"While Cilicia was flourishing, first the Fatimids, then the Seljuk Turks took Jerusalem and destroyed Christian holy places. The destruction of the Holy Sepulchre, which you just visited, in 1071 prompted the first crusade in 1099. The Armenians welcomed the Europeans and helped as best they could."

The Patriarch stood to show Mark a framed document from Pope Gregory XIII's *Ecclesia Romana* that read:

"Among the good deeds which the Armenian people has done towards the church and the Christian world, it should especially be stressed that, in those times when the

Christian princes and the warriors went to retake the Holy Land, no people or nation, with the same enthusiasm, joy and faith came to their aid as the Armenians did, who supplied the Crusaders with horses, provisions and guidance. The Armenians assisted these warriors with their utter courage and loyalty during the Holy wars."

Beside this inscription was a reproduction of a painting by Henri Delaborde from 1844 showing Constantine III of Armenia on his throne with a Hospitaller.

The Patriarch continued. "For two hundred years, the struggle for control of the Holy Land ensued through seven major crusades and several minor ones until the complete Crusader withdrawal in 1291. This left Crusader states and a Crusader presence adjacent to Cilician Armenia and at other strategic points in the region, including the island of Cyprus. Guy of Lusignan, who had been the Crusader King of Jerusalem, bought Cyprus from England's King Richard I after the Crusades, eventually passing the title for the island to Venice, which is important because the Lusignan dynasty also included Armenian kings. The Armenians became Westernized and close to Roman Catholicism, though the Armenian Church maintained its independence. The Mekhitarist Order is Armenian Catholic—they have a monastery and publishing house here in Jerusalem. Ours was the very first, however.

"Cilicia eventually fell to Mamluk attacks mounted from Egypt in 1375, but those of means had already relocated across Europe and around the world by then. The seat of the Armenian Church was restored to Holy Echmiadzin in 1441, but an independent Catholicos remained in Cilicia, at St. Sophia in Sis. He fled in the 1915 genocide along with those who'd managed to survive the horror. Since 1930, the Catholicos of the House of Cilicia is located in Antelias, Lebanon."

Jamison raised his eyebrows and exhaled a sigh of mental exhaustion. "I understand now about the history of playing chess in real life and playing off multiple opponents in a circular setting. I guess that is Byzantine chess, after all."

"Now, about the secrets—clearly, there are many of them. My guess is that they all went to Europe before Byzantium and Cilicia fell, probably in the 1200s. At that time, Venice was the fastest rising European power and offered the greatest sanctuary in its lagoon. Again, this is only my opinion. Certainly the Mekhitarists at San Lazaro have a magnificent storage facility with an enormous amount of manuscripts and documents, but secrets related to chess would have come with travelers on the caravans or maybe through a royal gift in exchange for favors in the days of Tigranes the Great, possibly even before his time. I have heard both about matters being settled with chess over the years and about secret plays that were not shared with others as the game was being developed. This would certainly make sense with Byzantine chess, but here, I think you must visit Holy Echmiadzin and the official archival repository, the Matenadaran of Yerevan, to learn more."

As the Patriarch finished speaking, Mark pulled a small, purple velvet pouch containing a single gold coin from his pocket and handed it to the Patriarch. It was the coin Putin had given his son in Salzburg.

"Have you ever seen either of the depictions on this coin?"

The Patriarch studied the coin carefully and examined both sides.

"Mark, I won't ask you where this came from because it is obviously recently minted and not original."

"Any idea of who is depicted?"

"One side looks to me like a reproduction of a gold solidus of Byzantine Emperor Heraclius, who was an Armenian—that is to say, his parents were Armenian. The other is a depiction of a pope from Rome. You'll need to confirm this, of course."

"What do you make of it, Surpazan Hayr?"

"Heraclius ruled in the 600s. He drove the Persians out of Asia Minor and defeated their king in Ninevah, then turned to Roman Catholic Pope John IV and worked with him to convert the Balkans to Christianity. Heraclius worked to end the schisms that developed among the early Christian churches and corresponded with the Muslim prophet named Muhammed."

"So, he defended the Christians and then sought to unite them and spread the faith. I'll bet the back of the coin depicts Pope John IV, the other half of that relationship."

"That certainly would make sense. I agree."

"Well, if I told you the coin came from a Russian, what sense would that make?"

"Well, of course, Russia didn't exist at that time, but the idea of the Byzantine East working closely with the Roman West to spread Christianity to the Slavs would certainly make sense to today's Russians. It would make sense to anyone who wants to close ranks and march ahead together, in fact. The idea of a Christian reaching out to the Prophet Muhammed has to appeal to anyone who wants a universal understanding of monotheism, as well.

"I think Churchill described Russia as a riddle wrapped in a mystery inside an enigma. He was really referring to the Byzantine mentality, and Armenia has had a lot of experience dealing with it—just maybe, we are the source of some of it. Take your Byzantine chess, for example. If your coin really does show Heraclius playing Byzantine chess, the Russians, of all people, would understand its meaning."

"Surpazan Hayr, I am indebted to you for this visit and for your willingness to impart your knowledge and thoughts. Archbishop Atemian thought that I may also be of some small assistance to you, in return."

"Mark, the situation in Karabagh is our number-one priority. We can't let more massacres of innocent Armenians by Turks go on. I have tried to get the authorities here to speak out, both on the Genocide and on what is taking place today, but this country favors Turkey in all matters, even silencing talk of Turkey's bloody past. You are in a position to speak out and to help, so you must do so. Speak also of what you have seen here and of how difficult the authorities make things for us. You now know this place's full history. We have gotten on with Persians, Arabs, Fatimids, Byzantines, Turks, the British, and now the Israelis. We have to fight to keep every inch of space. When we can't maintain that space, we fall into jeopardy of losing it to the authorities—the same ones who won't give us a permit to make repairs in the first place. And so it goes. Did someone tell you the Byzantine Empire had ended?…Maybe it has taken over the entire planet.

"I have old friends at the Matenadaran, and of course Echmiadzin will be open fully to you when you arrive there. Travel safely to Yerevan, and pass along my warmest greetings to our Vehapar, the Catholicos. Please take these gifts with you. Is your dear mother Anush still with us? One of these is for her."

"Thank you again, Surpazan Hayr. This will mean so much to her, as our visit has meant so much to me. I hope we meet again to celebrate peace in the world and maybe a final end to the need for a Byzantine mentality."

"But only after you learn all of the Byzantine's secrets, Mark, and put them to good use." The Patriarch smiled. "Bedros will arrange your connections to Yerevan. Enjoy your evening here in the Quarter and don't let the ringing of our bells keep you awake. Also, please let me know how you find things in Yerevan and Echmiadzin. Be aware, though—the conditions are miserable. They had to close the nuclear power station, which was modeled on Chernobyl. The socialist economy is shattered, and the capitalist one is very rudimentary. Be sure to take some extra food in your suitcase. God bless you, Mark."

"And you as well, Surpazan Hayr."

CHAPTER
17

Yerevan, Armenia

The itinerary provided by the Patriarchate had Jamison transiting through Athens and spending the better part of a full day in airports to get to Yerevan. Getting through the new Republic of Armenia's Szvartnotz International Airport was grueling, too. He was waiting in the VIP lounge and was reminded of his special status for the three hours he was ignored there before his visa would be examined for entry. When he finally made it out of the airport, the taxi to Republic Square had enough second-hand cigarette smoke in it to be first-hand. The evening in a cold room with the famous Russian chandelier (a bare light bulb hanging from the ceiling) at his hotel had him questioning the wisdom of his visit.

His visit to the main cathedral of Armenia, built in 301 AD, was enough to quiet his concerns, however. In the museum underneath were artifacts defying credibility. One claimed to be the Roman spear that pierced the side of Jesus of Nazareth during his crucifixion. The museum also claimed to have a piece of Noah's Ark that had been carried down from Mt. Ararat, which lay at the center of Armenia's historic homeland.

The local version of history, based on early historical accounts, archeology, and legend, had the Armenians as descendants of a grandson of Noah named Haik—they sometimes called themselves "Hyes" in honor of this ancestry. They were another "chosen people" who were to repopulate the earth and destroy the evils of Babylon. Interestingly, archeology has turned up nothing to deny the legend of the flood, which appeared in the earliest texts of many cultures. To the contrary, archeologists have continued to roll back the clock for this people, whose origins appear lost in the mists of prehistory.

Following a brief introduction to the venerated Catholicos of all Armenians, a young celibate priest named Father Hovsep was assigned to take Mark to their library and archives. He was selected because of his English skills and his degree in history from Tufts University, which he obtained prior to entering the seminary in Evanston, Illinois and coming to Echmiadzin.

"So Mark, there are a few things I can mention at the outset," Father Hovsep began while escorting him. "You know a lot about 'recent' history, so maybe I'll go back a little further. Shatranj *is* the game that became chess, and you are right that its roots go to India and Persia—but to some extent, so do ours."

"I don't understand."

"You certainly know about Alexander the Great and his record of conquests. He crossed Armenia en route to India in 326 BC, and scores of Armenians went along with him on his journeys and remained both in India and Persia.

"The Hyes—the Armenians—had already been traders on the Malabar coast and elsewhere in India for 700 years when Vasco da Gama arrived in 1498. The Armenians were called the Merchant Princes of India in his time. By that time, we held many administrative, medical, and legal posts in India.

"When the English arrived in 1688, the local Armenians made them agree to build churches across India—one in every community in which at least forty Armenians were present—and they had to agree to pay the priestly salaries. With this understanding, the Hyes helped them start the English East India Company, and many became very English in the process. Sir Paul Chater, for example, who left Kolkata to develop Hong Kong, was born Khatchik Boghos Astwachatoor.

"Outside of India, the Hyes were based in Persia, with New Julfa, near Isfahan, as the most populous center although most didn't arrive there until the seventeenth century. That's where the Hye brothers who created the Raffles Hotel in Singapore were from."

Mark felt compelled to chime in. "It's still considered one of the best hotels. Of course, I'm sure it's no match for where I stayed last night." He couldn't control the sarcasm in his voice at this last statement.

"Were you okay, Mark? We can always put you up here, you know. We would be very happy to."

"No, it's really alright. This transition is hard on everyone, and I shouldn't be made too comfortable while most people here are without energy and food. Before my arrival, reports told me that nearly all the trees have been cut for firewood and that there is widespread deprivation. I saw signs of it coming in from the airport."

"There is actual starvation here, Mark. We are blockaded by Turkey and Azerbaijan, and they are keeping out our purchases and international food relief intended to reach us. Let people know that when you return home."

"I promise."

After a pause in which both men looked deeply into the eyes of the other, Father Hovsep went on to a new subject. "Are you curious about the old Silk Road?"

"We all learn in school about Marco Polo traveling along the Silk Road to the court of Kubla Khan in Xanadu, but I'm always interested in learning more," Mark responded, knowing he was about to learn a great deal more.

Father Hovsep explained, "He came through Armenia and described in his writings many Armenian trading centers for a long distance on the way to China. Many think the

West created the road to get to China's goods—especially silk, of course—but trading with China through the Silk Road was initiated not by the West, but by China as a matter of deliberate policy initiated by Zhang Qian in the second century BC. Chang'an, today's Xi'an, was the largest and most advanced city in the world at the time of the creation of the trade route, and it served as the terminus of the Silk Road."

"I have been there," Mark proclaimed. "To say it was advanced is an understatement. They were literally 1,000 years ahead of Europe in many technologies. In 200 BC, they had chromed swords that still haven't shown signs of rust today. The West didn't develop those until the eighteenth century. The terracotta soldiers in Xi'an were unbelievable, too, but I know that only a relatively small number have been unearthed. The emperor's tomb, described in ancient texts, remains covered. Unlike the West, which rushes ahead with everything immediately, the Chinese have learned patience. They are waiting for the right time to uncover it, for their ancient treasures to be properly appreciated by their people and the world."

"Some technologies were shared, some were sold, and some remained secret," Father Hovsep continued.

"Technologies that could be used to destroy one's enemies, like Greek fire or many other techniques used to hold the Turks at bay for as long as possible?"

"Correct. Everything that had value could be traded, but some things were beyond value, or the correct value wouldn't be found until the circumstances warranted."

Mark remembered what Hani had said and added, "Sometimes it wasn't technology at all that was traded or guarded, but how to think and view situations strategically, like the Chinese game of Go, which was not always about confronting situations directly, as in Western chess and thinking."

"Correct again, Mark. Commerce on the road was expanded through the Han Dynasty, which fought wars and put down rebellions to ensure peace and attract trade along this important route. Caravan traffic reached its peak with the Tang Dynasty in 600 AD, leading to the rapid development of China's economy and society. The opposite end of the Silk Road at that time lay in Armenia, in the hands of Byzantine Emperors like Justinian and Heraclius, who welcomed the expansion and began introducing silk to the newly retaken Roman lands in Western Europe, including those retaken for the Byzantines by General Nerses."

Mark raised a finger to catch Father Hovsep's attention before he continued. He reached for his gold coin and handed it to Father Hovsep, relating all that the Patriarch of Jerusalem had shared a few days before.

"Yes, Archbishop Munushian has always been one of our most well-informed clergy members. I would certainly say he is quite correct in his assumptions concerning this coin," confirmed Father Hovsep. "You know, Emperor Heraclius is one of the most revered emperors in the East, yet little is known of him in the West. He ended corruption in the government of the empire and reorganized the military and public administration, which allowed him to win incredible victories. He adopted Greek instead of Latin as the official language of the empire. When he defeated the Persian king Khosrau, Heraclius was able to recover the True Cross of our Lord from the Persians, who had transported it to Ninevah. Heraclius returned it triumphantly to Jerusalem and has been depicted as a hero in countless works of art ever since."

"He was actually an Armenian by birth?" Mark asked, seeking confirmation of what the Patriarch had said.

"Ten Roman emperors came into this world from Armenian parents and considered themselves as such, though entirely loyal to Byzantium. Heraclius was among them.

"So as I was saying about the Silk Road—it was 600 years later that the Venetian Marco Polo set forth from Armenia along the well-established route to begin his famous service in the court of Kubla Khan, finding the Mongol emperor at his summer residence in Xanadu. This Khan, the grandson of Genghis Khan, was curious about developments in the West, and Polo became his emissary. Marco Polo was allowed to return to Venice with the Khan's request to return with 100 Catholic priests. When he returned, he carried a letter from the Roman Catholic Pope. The priests rebelled along the arduous journey and returned to the comforts of home, but Polo returned for more adventures in a period of service to Kubla Khan that occupied seventeen years."

They had reached the library, and Father Hovsep left Mark to his studies.

Jamison found his visits at Echmiadzin and the Matenateran in Yerevan as fascinating as they were dark and cold. After two days and a brain full of facts and stories he considered historical treasures, he left with no real answers about a secret archive related to chess or any variation of the game. The half of him that was Armenian and normally taken for granted now lit up like a burning ember within him.

CHAPTER

18

London—1991

Jamison flew directly from Yerevan to London for a teaching commitment at the Inns of Court School of Law at Gray's Inn, just off High Holborn. Sarah dutifully gathered up Mark's books and teaching materials from the castle, packed a suitcase for him, and brought the children along to join him at the old residence halls of Regent's College, where they all preferred staying. The refectory there served leeks and had an abundance of Coleman's mustard. The staff showered great affection on him and his family, doubtless owing to the difference of his personality and the majority of faculty who passed through, showing themselves to be pompous asses that ordered the staff around like their personal servants.

Sarah and the children loved the Queen Mary Rose Garden and strolling in the parks, and the open-air Shakespeare theatre suited the young family perfectly. He enjoyed taking the Tube from Baker Street and transferring at Oxford Circus to get to Holborn. It was a fine contrast to life at the castle and a pleasant respite from all the attentiveness of a staff of forty.

While walking back from class one day, he decided to detour from his usual route and visit the British Museum on Great Russell Street. Touring the galleries, he looked in vain for the section on Armenia and found instead a glossed-over history of the region in a section called "Ancient Turkey," which required some further examination and reflection on his part because there was no such thing as "ancient" Turkey. Turkey was a modern state whose people only arrived on the scene in Anatolia relatively recently.

He started to reflect on what he had recently learned in Jerusalem and Yerevan. The English, and later the British Empire, really began their colonization efforts with the Armenians at nearly every point, whether in the Middle East, Persia, India, and beyond. The Armenians had established commercial communities throughout the regions going back 2,000 years—more in some cases. The Turkish Petroleum Company, which became the Iraq Petroleum Company, and the Anglo-Persian Oil Company ran into a problem with Calouste Gulbenkian holding all the oil and mineral rights in the region they wanted to work in. The international arbitrations filled many shelves at law school libraries.

Perhaps the British Museum, like the British leaders in the Crimean War era, preferred to erase the Armenians altogether. Certainly Turkey would be glad of that; it was cleaner and easier for them to just disregard the fact that anyone was there first and avoid issues of rights and legitimate titles to things. In the case of the British, maybe it was easier not to acknowledge the senior partner in expansion endeavors, who was tossed out the boardroom window at the earliest opportunity after all usefulness was extracted. No wonder Parliamentary debate had been particularly tough over the Foreign Office decision to join the Turks, who were in the process of slaughtering Christian minorites.

Despite this, in each case of British commercial and later imperial expansion, the Armenians welcomed their fellow Christians into an inhospitable region of the world and launched their enterprises and administrations successfully. In each case, it seemed, when the opportunity arose, the British turned on the Armenians and facilitated their demise. Now, Mark Jamison found himself eyeball-to-signpost with the ultimate insult of all. "Ancient Turkey," indeed! What the hell happened to Armenia as "the cradle of civilization?" Did history only remember the destroyers of civilizations, not the builders? All the attention that had been given to the Mongols and Turks, and what, exactly, had they contributed? Putting up a minaret beside the most beautiful church in Christendom and covering over the intricate Byzantine iconography inside the Hagia Sophia, the Holy Wisdom of God? That trip to the British Museum got Jamison's hackles up, and then some.

When he calmed down, he reflected on the Great Game that the US took on from the British and the idea of using locals in an area of interest as pawns on a chessboard. It didn't work in the long run. It was the wrong game altogether. It was the game to end empires, not build them, to end friendships, not build them. Would the US follow Britain's lead and erase or alter history to suit itself as well? The US didn't officially recognize the genocide of nearly two million Armenians, whose slaughter was the example articulated when the United Nations created the very term "genocide" in 1946.

What a convenient game this Great Game is, Mark thought, *when reality can be as easily distorted as history can be rewritten.*

At the beginning of class the next day, Mark Jamison threw the chalkboards up on the elevated platform at Gray's Inn. The students were all lawyers from around the world who were there to learn about financing large international commercial transactions and projects, a course he had introduced here based on his work with USAID. He had a particularly challenging group and appreciated that they kept him on his toes. "The best way to learn is to teach" was a favored mantra of his.

As he turned back toward the class, he happened to glance at the normally empty gallery that hung above the rear of the lecture hall. Its sole occupant was Malcolm Wyle, who was attentively listening to him. After class, Wyle waited for him. They slipped away to Holborn and turned right, heading up the block to the Bung Hole Pub to catch up.

Wyle was in town working with Domich&Carey's London team on a deal involving both Bechmann Engineering and the Xinjiang D'Fray Group. He wasn't at liberty to provide details, but it was fairly clear from what he could say that it involved a new pipeline deal.

They decided to meet for dinner that night at Wyle's hotel. The Connaught was generally thought to be financially out of reach to most, even on an ambassador's salary, so Domich&Carrey had to be treating him well. Sarah was going to join them, so two of Mark's students who were also staying at Regents College volunteered to watch the children for a few hours, benefitting from a large package of cookies and favorable recognition from the children's father.

The Connaught was near the US Embassy in Grosvenor Square, a place both Mark and Wyle knew and cherished as part of "old, snobby London." Jamison remembered a colleague telling him that Cary Grant used to stay at the Connaught when he was in town, while Fred Astaire would stay at the Savoy. The difference said a great deal about any occupant, including Malcolm Wyle. The Savoy was loud, while the Connaught was immensely quiet and understated. Jamison loved the full tails worn by the staff at the Connaught and how the cigars were presented and prepared.

Malcolm hosted the dinner with a good champagne and Bordeaux that accompanied a fine fish and game course, followed by a cherries jubilee and Courvoisier. During the dinner, Mark was even able to enjoy his beloved leeks. He still felt that Wyle was trying to recruit him for Domich&Carey, and was suspicious that the man was now out to win Sarah over to the possibility. Jamison didn't think that Wyle would be interested in his recent travels and visits, or that he would even know about them, but somehow he did. Wyle quickly brought up the games Hani had described a long while back in Oman and announced that if there was anything Jamison had uncovered during his visits, Wyle's clients in Xinjiang wanted to know.

Mark described the difficult circumstances he'd encountered in landlocked and blockaded Armenia, and Wyle seemed vaguely interested, but largely indifferent. Wyle talked about his frequent trips to Baku, and Mark quickly understood that Domich&Carey was negotiating a pipeline deal on behalf of Bechmann that involved Azerbaijan.

Jamison wondered if Wyle knew anything about the Armenians inside Azerbaijan and the recent massacres. If Wyle had any sympathy for the Karabagh Armenians breaking free from both the Soviets and the Azeris, he revealed little of it, asking only if Mark had ever heard of *Nabucco*?

"You mean the Verdi opera? *Nabucco* is the Italian name for Nebuchadnezzar, the Babylonian king. The opera libretto says he freed the Israelites from their enslavement, which is incorrect. It was really the Persian king Cyrus the Great who did this sometime later, after Cyrus conquered Babylon. Great opera, though."

"Well, I suspect you'll be hearing more about this name, and it won't relate to an opera or to misstated ancient history."

"What, then?"

"You and Sarah are living in Austria now, aren't you? You should ask the Austrians—and if you do, please tell them that Bechmann is up to the job."

"Are you going to leave it at that? You must be talking about a pipeline. Based on what you've said this evening, the pipeline must be planned to connect Azerbaijan with Austria, but is that even possible? That's an enormous distance."

"You have no idea what this will do to the Russians! They will be livid, so let's keep it between ourselves for now and see how it develops...I haven't been ignoring your concern for the Armenians and the situation in Nagorno Karabagh tonight, by the way. There is someone I might introduce you to tomorrow after your class. Would you be free if I came by and walked you over to meet him?"

"Sarah, you wouldn't mind missing me a little more than usual tomorrow afternoon, would you?"

"Not if it helps you relax a bit about the British and concentrate a bit more on your family," she replied, smiling.

Mark reached across the table for Sarah's hand and sent a kiss and wink of appreciation her way. He then turned and nodded to Malcolm. "See you after class."

19

The following day, Mark kept an eye peeled for Wyle, but Jamison didn't see him until he'd finished with the students who lined his path heading out to High Holborn to ask him questions. He turned right and nearly ran over Malcolm as the former ambassador hurried over to meet him.

"Sorry I'm a bit late—Bechmann meetings."

"Not a problem. Where are we heading?"

"It's just five minutes from here. It's a small office with a gentleman you will find interesting."

They headed up High Holborn and turned on Southhampton Place, then walked along Bloomsbury Square Garden for a short distance. It was a route familiar to Mark; they were heading very near to the British Museum. When they passed in front of an old, nondescript entryway on Montague Street, Wyle stopped and indicated they should go inside. A small, dark lobby and an elevator, or lift as the Londoners call them, was summoned by Wyle, who pushed for the fourth floor. When they got out, a number of stenciled glass doors greeted them on either side of the narrow hallway. They proceeded to one bearing the name "Anglo-Xinjiang Alliance."

The entry contained a worn brown leather sofa, two plain wooden chairs, and an end table with a dim lamp. Wyle knocked on the inside door and Jamison heard a curt, "Yeah, come in."

Wyle stepped inside and shook hands with the sole occupant, who rose and walked in front of his desk to meet Mark. "Franz, this is the gentleman I told you about, Mark Jamison. Mark, Franz Gottlieb."

Mark's mind started racing. Franz was F.C. Gottlieb, the coin dealer from Washington, DC whom he'd spotted with Wyle at Old Ebbitt Grill. Things were definitely getting more interesting regarding this pipeline.

"Mr. Gottlieb," Mark said by way of introduction, "unless I'm very mistaken, I met you before, when you were a rare coin dealer on M Street in DC."

Wyle intervened before Gottlieb could respond. "Mark, he works for us and wears several identities. He is also the executive director of the Anglo-Xinjiang Alliance. Using his various roles, Franz tends to meet people we are interested in."

"I thought you retired from all this, Malcolm. Aren't you a partner with Domich&Carey now?"

Gottlieb piped up. "Of course he is, Mark, just like you're a professor this week. Sometimes who we really work for can get confusing, but you know as much about all that as anyone."

"Mark, Mr. Gottlieb is Turkish. We have been borrowing him for the past five years or so...Actually, we share him with the British. When I mentioned your concerns about the treatment of your mother's relatives, he asked to share a few things with you, and I wanted to join you and see what I could learn, too, if that's okay with both of you."

"Of course," Gottlieb agreed as he motioned for them to be seated.

"Maybe the best way for me to start my story is with another story," Gottlieb began. "Have either of you read *Greenmantle*? It was first published as a work of fiction by John Buchan in 1916, but it reveals a bit of reality that many still don't want to discuss, and certainly not my countrymen in Turkey. The upshot of the story is that the last Ottoman sultan couldn't be pressured to do a few things the Western governments wanted, so a new "progressive" leadership was brought in who called themselves the Young Turks—Enver, Talaat, and Jemal. They weren't really Muslims and weren't really Turks. The book asks how Enver, a Polish adventurer, and a collection of Jews and gypsies could have gained control of the empire, then dismisses the obvious answer—it was done with German organization, arms, and money.

"The end of the Ottoman Empire and the beginning of modern Turkey were riddled with spies and intrigue, foreign interests, foreign investments, and political aspirations from outside. Even Ataturk's origins are opaque, as were those of a cadre of leaders extending all the way to Erdogan. These leaders subordinated Turkish identity and culture for modernity at a price that included continuing foreign intrigue and making Turkey a central figure in the chessboard of the Great Game.

"The Young Turks came to power with the support of the pro-Western intellectuals inside Turkey who had been very sadly deceived. Tragically, this included the Armenians. I say 'tragically' because the agenda of the Young Turks, brought in by the West, included ruthlessly removing any possible impingement on the flow of oil from Baku to Batumi and any excuse for Russian protection of its fellow Christians—this was the one thing the British, Germans, and French could agree upon once the French Rothschilds took a position in Baku. The only benign part of their agenda was the establishment of a Jewish home in Palestine. The British and Americans took the lead on this project with Enver even though the murder of the Armenian nation was in full progress during the negotiations.

"The last leg of the Berlin-Baghdad Railway was opened with deportations of Armenians to the hinterlands, where they were disposed of. It was a lesson that was not lost on Hitler. He reacted to the fears of his general staff over getting away with a similar fate for the Jews with that famous quote, 'Who today remembers the Armenians?'

"Many in Turkey are livid at the continuing denials by our government, Britain, and the USA concerning the historical record. We know what happened, we just haven't come to grips with how it happened and why it happened. We haven't figured out who we are as a people and a country. Do the founders of modern Turkey include Jews disguised as Muslims who incited a jihad—a Holy War—by Kurds and Turks against their Christian neighbors and long-standing friends? Was the incitement the work of Germany? In *Greenmantle*, the mastermind was a German woman. Turkey's historical record bears support for such a figure.

"I tell you all this so that you know who killed your mother's relatives and countrymen. It was the Great Game that killed the Armenians. It is the Great Game that continues to kill them and vast numbers of others who find themselves caught as pawns of the major powers on the chessboard."

Malcolm Wyle looked expectantly at Mark for some reaction to what Gottlieb had said.

"Mr. Gottlieb, I'm going to guess that your family was composed of German Jews who managed to escape the madness in the thirties by coming to Turkey," Mark ventured.

"Like the Jews who fled the Spanish inquisition in an earlier century—some of their descendants are among those I just spoke of," answered Gottlieb.

"So what is the answer to this madness? Is the Anglo-Xinjiang Alliance helping to resolve it or perpetuate it? You can't possibly have a role in *Nabucco*, can you? It's a pipeline to Europe."

"And if there are snags, the pipeline will go eastward to Urumqi. There are no losers on this one."

"And if Muslim fundamentalists get in the way of the pipeline?" Jamison inquired.

"No one will get in the way of the pipeline."

"I think I just listened to you speak about that scenario a few moments ago."

Malcolm Wyle spoke up. "Nothing's different now—just more money involved."

F.C. Gottlieb sat silently, looking Mark over in the same way he had during their first meeting at the coin shop.

"Listen, Mr. Gottlieb—if that is your real name—everything you said is appreciated and helpful in understanding the past, but your fellow Turks are at it again. Armenians are being murdered in their ancient homeland of Karabagh, and those inside the new republic of Armenia are freezing and starving because of the Turkish blockade. Turkey and Armenia are supposedly at peace, but the Turks are still killing Armenians. Turkey steals food aid shipments coming from the United States to help the Armenians. Tell me: Do you have any influence in Ankara or in Baku?"

"Some."

"Can you do anything to stop this insanity? Can you get the blockade lifted or help with a ceasefire?"

"Maybe."

"What does 'maybe' mean?"

"What do you offer in return? Do you have anything to trade? I understand you have been digging around in Armenian archives and repositories. Have you found something buried there that would be of value?"

Wyle interjected, "Maybe something that might relate to our meeting in Oman."

"Or maybe something the Chinese might think is rightfully theirs," Gottlieb suggested.

Jamison was stunned at both the questions and how closely his activities had been followed. "What *could* you be talking about?"

"The Chinese tell me something of priceless value was lost on the way to the Vatican a very long time ago, back in Marco Polo's day," Gottlieb shared.

"Or even long before that," Wyle finished for him.

Mark Jamison thought carefully about how he should respond before slowly rising to his feet. "Well, gentlemen, this has certainly been interesting. I will give thought to everything said and the propositions made in this room. Mr.

Gottlieb, do you actually know anything about ancient coins?"

Gottlieb responded proudly, "I'm also an assistant curator across the street. I'm the British Museum's rare and ancient coin consultant."

"Bet that lets you into some interesting places around the world." With that, Mark shook hands with Gottlieb and Wyle and departed, closing the door behind him.

Gottlieb looked doubtfully at Wyle. "I personally find all of this hard to believe, Malcolm. Do you think he may actually be onto something?"

"I'll stay on him."

CHAPTER

20

Mark Jamison left Gottlieb's office needing a drink....A stiff double or two, actually.

He waved down a taxi and headed for the Savoy Hotel's lounge. He could drink anywhere in London, but it had been many years since his last visit to the Savoy.

"Too modern now," he muttered to himself upon entering the hotel. He found his way to the bar, sat on a glorified high chair, and ordered a double Laphroaig neat, being his usual preoccupied and unobservant self. When he shook himself free of his thoughts long enough to look around, he turned his head to the right at the precise moment that a head holding a lovely pair of eyes turned to the left and met his. Maybe she had been looking at him since he sat down—he didn't know. In either case, she had some of the largest and prettiest penetrating green eyes he had ever enjoyed being undressed with. They were surrounded by a pert, inquisitive face that shined with intelligent curiosity and was topped with well-styled boyish auburn hair that dropped ever-so slightly in the direction of her upturned nose. She had a complexion as fair as the clotted cream the English loved so dearly. Now he understood why they loved it so much.

"Do we know each other?" she asked demurely.

"I certainly hope so. Are you a lawyer, by any chance?"

"Can't stand them."

"Ah. Me neither. Lousy bunch. That's certainly in your favor...I was just testing you."

She continued to gaze at him in a way that drew his chair toward hers with a force vastly more powerful and unobtrusive than gravity itself.

"Well, what do you do, lovely lady of the Savoy?"

"Many things, mysterious gentleman who intrigues me...Many things in many places."

"How about naming one or two? You know, you look familiar to me, as well. I thought it was just wishful thinking."

"Well, I fly airplanes."

"Out of Kenya?"

"Long time ago."

He pushed his chair next to hers. "Excuse me for a moment." He brushed his nose along her neck and breathed the scent that had always stayed with him. "I could never forget this perfume."

"I don't wear perfume."

"Then I need one more pass at you." This time, he lightly kissed her neck and then looked into her eyes and very gently brushed his lips against hers. "Do you remember me now?"

"The night we nearly flattened out on the escarpment! Of course I remember you."

"I must be certain," Jamison said as he again nuzzled her neck and ran his tongue along it. This time he got a giggle and a push away.

"Damn right I remember that tongue. Does it come with a name?"

"Excuse me. Yes, of course. Mark Jamison. And you are?"

"Carol Durlen. Used to be Carol Hardy Durlen. Carol Hardy when I met you...You sure hire large planes to haul you around."

"It's a long story. Let me get you another drink."

"Just one—I'm meeting friends pretty soon."

"One is enough. Why did you run away that night? I tried to find you, but you vanished as soon as we landed."

"In case you couldn't guess, I nearly soiled my trousers when we clipped those trees. When I started back to the office, the goons were already all over you. I couldn't interfere or I'd risk my job. I did think about you, though. Really I thought of you for a long while. I called you some weeks later, but the embassy said you'd left. I figured Rainbow Aviation was something you'd rather forget about—this bush pilot included. Pity, really. I could have used the company."

"Well, I missed you the whole time I was there. Your scent was magical. You are still magical. What do you do now? Other than smelling wonderful at the Savoy, that is."

"I'm still flying. Right now it's mostly charters for oil executives and their prospectors to Central Asia. Some go over there calling themselves art dealers, but I know they're looting the place of any cultural artifacts and treasures they can make off with rather than dealing in art. The locals are all crooked and will sell anything for the right price."

"Ever fly Bechmann Engineering folks over there?"

"All the time. Victor Domich is one of my favorite passengers, and he's often with them. I'm making a lot of runs to Kazakhstan, and sometimes on from there to Urumqi in Xinjiang. Domich is another lawyer, like you—I didn't believe your BS about them. I remember how confident you were about your charter way back in Nairobi. Victor Domich is like you in many ways."

"Well, I can't fault his choice of pilots. We seem to have similar tastes."

She gave Mark a sudden glance that said a great deal: She was having an affair with the founding partner of one of the most powerful law firms in the world, which was interested in recruiting him. Working for Domich&Carey didn't seem like such a bad idea at that moment.

"Does Domich spend much time in Xinjiang?"

"I overhear him talk about the Anglo-Xinjiang Alliance and about the Uighurs. I think if the authorities won't give Bechmann the deal Domich&Carey wants for them, Victor will work on changing the authorities. He would be a tough one to cross."

As she finished her sentence, Carol looked to the entrance and saw a Chinese couple awaiting her. "My company this evening," she explained. "Victor wants me to dine with them and take them to the Shafesbury for theater afterward. See the fun you'll miss?"

"Maybe one day I can catch a lift with you again. This time, let's swap cards and stay in touch. Would that be okay with Victor?" he teased.

"It would be okay with *me*. Thanks for the drink," she chirped as she passed her card to him.

They stood and nodded their farewells, looking deeply in each other's eyes but not kissing goodbye with the Chinese couple watching her. Jamison sat back down and finished his drink before heading back to Sarah and the kids at Regents. There would be time for him to read bedtime stories then have a quiet dinner with Sarah when he got home.

CHAPTER

21

When his teaching stint in London concluded, Mark and his family returned to Salzburg and the myriad cares of a world in transition. The demise of the Soviet Union was only the beginning of changes to the world order. The invasion of Kuwait and expulsion of Iraqi forces, the advent of suicide bombers, and the expansion of fighting in Nagorno Karabagh all required his attention. He advised government leaders, lectured on the topics, wrote articles, and conducted seminar sessions. He helped the fledgling Republic of Armenia deal with its blockade by increasing food self-sufficiency and helping to organize a project called Winter Rescue. Through it all, he felt the inescapable tide of history washing over him and all his best efforts. The world was becoming more dangerous, not less, and the major players had grown even less caring about the pawns on the global chessboard.

Jamison searched in vain for some indication that his mysterious friend Hani Waladoon had understood the urgency of the letter he had sent many months before, watching and waiting for a sign. In May of 1994, there was a sudden breakthrough and ceasefire in Karabagh. Everything about it conveyed the handiwork of the Game Master: There had been an outside intervention cloaked in secrecy leading to a kind of swift resolution and capitulation in an otherwise intractable standoff.

Mark stayed close to Archbishop Scheuer and, through him, Cardinal Ratzinger, but their exchanges focused on broad topics. After the Karabagh ceasefire came an immediate shift of his attention to the carnage of the Hutus against the Tutsis in Rwanda, and after that there was the issue of how to deal with the Christian Serbs seen to be the aggressors in the Balkans. On it went. The increase in terrorism directed against the USA culminated in the September 11, 2001 attacks, and the Vatican was very interested in knowing how Mark had anticipated the targeting of New York's Twin Towers by hijacked aircraft.

Jamison never forgot the admonitions of Archbishops Atemian and Der Munushian to continually arouse the interest of the Vatican in chess and the secrecy surrounding the lost Byzantine treasures, so bits and pieces of these secrets found their way into correspondence fairly regularly. What he really wanted, though, was Hani's help in ferreting out where the real secrets lay and employing them for the benefit of all people compelled to suffer fates not of their choosing.

Mark also stayed in contact with Malcolm Wyle, though in some years, that contact came only in the form of the perfunctory Domich&Carey holiday card with an inserted typed message. The subject of Hani Waladoon was only addressed between them indirectly, and usually with the question, "Have you seen or heard from him?"

Mark put Carol Durlen out of his thoughts after that brief stint in London, especially after relocating with his family back to California. He wished he could say he kept her entirely out of his thoughts, but there was something there that he couldn't clearly articulate, even to himself.

The years went by, and finally a signal from Hani emerged in May of 2005, shortly after Cardinal Ratzinger was inaugurated as Pope Benedict XVI. The signal came from an unlikely figure, but one unmistakably close to the Game Master.

PART IV

CHAPTER

22

Urumqi, Xinjiang, China—2005

Jamison had promised himself the whole way across the Pacific that he would be careful what he ate or drank in China. He hadn't been on the ground more than half an hour and strangers in the transit lounge dining room were already shoving chopsticks in his face.

"You must try the local delicacies before you climb aboard the connecting flight to Urumqi," one person demanded.

"No, really—no thank you...What is that?"

"Rat intestine. During the Cultural Revolution, we learned to eat things like this and really acquired a taste for it—also many bugs. You must try it."

"No, honestly."

Cups were filled with something Mark could only assume was alcohol, and someone across the circular table from him stood up and said how honored he was that the famous Mark Jamison would soon be crossing the Gobi Desert on his people's behalf.

"*Gam Bay*," the person exclaimed.

He cringed. This meant he had to stand and drain the foul liquor. He could compare the taste of it only to lighter fluid. "*Gam Bay*," he said, already feeling nauseated.

Who were these people, anyway? How could he have accepted an invitation from Li Jihua, someone he'd never even said "hello" to before? Mark knew that he'd accepted because Li was friends with Hani Waladoon, and Hani

Waladoon had been invisible and impossible for Mark Jamison to reach for the past decade.

Jamison was exhausted from his rushed preparations for the flight and having gotten no sleep the night preceding it. At least he could sleep on the flight across China, he thought.

News of flight delays was catastrophic, however. This meant more *Gam Bay* time and enduring strange people with missing teeth taking the chopsticks from their mouths and trying to stick them between his taut lips.

Finally, the host, or whoever he was, clapped his hands and everyone suddenly departed, leaving Mark totally alone, bewildered, drunk, and dead tired. He found his way to the departure gate and discovered another four-hour delay for his flight. This was sheer agony. When he finally climbed aboard, it was a completely full flight with some of the most obese Chinese people he had ever seen assembled in his immediate vicinity. The heavy aircraft lunged skyward, and his exhausted head bobbed forward. At precisely the same moment, the seat of the ample gentleman immediately in front of him thrust backward, rewarding Jamison with a face full of black hair that may or may not have been washed within the last month or so. He imagined its flavor to be about as tantalizing as the rat intestines.

Finally, after what seemed like several eternities, the plane was on the ground at his destination and a woman with a signboard was steering him along to transportation and a hotel bed. *Bed!*

He hit the pillow already unconscious. In what seemed one minute, but was actually two hours and twenty minutes, he answered a knock at the door and discovered several people in suits lined up in the hall and saying that he was keeping them waiting and that he had slept through breakfast. Welcome to Xinjiang!

Awake, dressed, and in the lobby and without coffee ("Chinese drink tea," he was often reminded), he was whisked aboard a minibus going…somewhere. The cigarette smoke mingled with the smog outside and the headache from the *Gam Bays* his brain refused to forget, however merciful forgetting might have been.

"Li Jihua?" Mark inquired, looking for the man who invited him to China and onto this minibus. "Mr. Li?"

The others aboard laughed. "Mr. Li," Mark emphasized. There was more laughter.

Finally they pulled up to a modern hotel building. The other passengers got out without a word, and a solitary figure wearing dark glasses stepped aboard. The minibus proceeded into the traffic without a word spoken by anyone, and the figure sat down immediately across from Jamison.

"Mark Jamison?"

"I firmly believe so. Yes," Mark responded. Coffee would have given him greater assurance in his response.

"I am Mr. Li."

Mark thought, *Central casting couldn't have done better,* but simply responded aloud, "Good morning, Mr. Li."

"It was very good of you to come all this way on short notice, especially since we've never actually met."

"I am pleased to meet you. I came because Hani Waladoon spoke highly of you."

"I'm afraid I don't know any such person."

Mark wanted to crawl back to the airport and depart from this nightmare. "Well, why did you ask to see me here? You said it was vitally important, and I thought it had to do with my old friend. Where are we going, by the way?"

"The reason for this visit is vitally important, I assure you."

Jamison felt like he was watching an old Charlie Chan film from the 1930s in which he was a bit actor.

"Did you know that Urumqi is the city furthest from any body of water?" Mr. Li offered.

This fact was just what Mark didn't want to hear. He grew up on the San Francisco Bay, joined the Navy to be on the water, and often found himself gazing endlessly at the rivers and canals coursing through Salzburg and at the small lake behind the castle when he'd lived there. The prospect of no water was as bad as the prospect of no coffee.

"Did you know that this was a major trading center on the old Silk Road? The caravans came through Kashgar and headed here on the way to Xi'an."

"Yes, I recall reading about that."

"Everyone, of course, remembers Marco Polo, who worked for the great Mongol lord Kubla Khan, the grandson of Genghis Khan."

"Of course." Mark wondered where this all was going.

"And that he was allowed to return to Venice with certain documents, invitations, and gifts from the Khan, all on the condition that he return to Xi'an."

"With 100 Catholic priests, as I recall."

"My, you certainly are well-read."

"You're not suggesting that this has anything to do with why I'm here, are you?"

"You know the new Pope, I am informed."

"Why on earth would you think that?"

"Mr. Jamison, we in China still want to be in communication with the Pope."

"Well, I think China has an embassy in Rome, and maybe even a representative to the Vatican."

"Come, now; you are missing my point."

"Which is what, please?"

"That we desire to open up channels of communication with the Pope through someone of established credibility such as yourself."

"And just who is 'we'?"

The van pulled up to a palatial residence. Guards were scurrying about with their cell phones in their hands.

"I will let your host introduce himself and explain this when we are inside. In case you are wondering about why it was important for you to be here today specifically, I can tell you that our president will be visiting Urumqi this afternoon. We arranged for you to attend his presentation and meet him afterward."

"That would certainly be an honor."

Jamison was escorted into a massive living room with a table bearing the most beautiful display of fresh fruit he had ever seen—better even than what he'd seen in California—including the fabled Hami melons, grapes, figs, pears, watermelon, cantaloupe, and berries of all varieties. As he continued to look down the line of fruits, he saw coffee. Yes, brewed coffee and milk! He already liked his host, whoever he turned out to be. He poured himself a cup of coffee and drank it immediately.

"Please help yourself, Mr. Jamison. Is the coffee to your liking?" Mr Li inquired.

"Seems to be doing the trick."

"I beg your pardon?"

"Yes, I think I am regaining consciousness."

In came a small man in a white suit with a white shirt, red tie, and brown shoes. Mark liked the outfit. The fellow had a very bloodshot left eye, probably from too many *Gam Bays* the night before. This man and Mr. Li exchanged a few minutes of indiscernible conversation, occasionally pointing in Mark's direction. Mark finished several slices of ice-cold Hami melon. When they were finished, the short gentleman stepped up to Mark and introduced himself as "Smith, Mr. Smith." *Not another one from central casting*, Mark groaned inwardly.

"Please sit and allow me to explain matters. I see you like our local fruit—please continue to enjoy the food and coffee while I speak."

Sure beats rat intestines and the taste of fat Chinese people's unwashed hair, Mark thought, restraining himself from saying it out loud.

"So, Mr. Li tells me you know about the old Silk Road. It went through Armenia, but I am sure you know that. You are part Armenian yourself, are you not?"

Mark stared at the bloodshot eye and didn't respond.

"We are convinced that messages and gifts intended for the Pope never reached him—messages and gifts of great importance, secrets of our science, arts, and medicine. Throughout our history, communication with the West has been troublesome."

"The only transfer of messages involving the Pope and China that I know about in the times of the Silk Road involved Marco Polo and Kubla Khan," Mark answered. "Surely you can't be referring to anything that old?"

"Ah, but I am, Mr. Jamison. That old, and even much older. Your people in Armenia controlled a crossroads for the world, a bridge from East to West. Maybe some things were not passed along as intended. Your people may have something that doesn't belong to them."

Jamison finally realized what the cryptic message he'd received from Mr. Li years earlier was about.

"Mr. Jamison, we know that you have been spending a lot of time over the years looking into whether or not a certain key related to the game of Byzantine chess may exist. We know you followed its trail to Jerusalem and Yerevan…Did you know that Kubla Khan was fascinated with this game?"

Jamison stared at Mr. Smith, or whatever his name was, and pursed his lower lip. "No."

"We think secrets about various board and strategy games were among the most highly prized treasures of the day. These games became a secret preserve of the ruling circles; mastering them was seen to be essential to the conduct of both diplomacy and warfare. We find ourselves once again turning to games and gaming theories today, but there are areas of game theory that even our super computers can't resolve, and there are pressing issues facing us now, especially here in Xinjiang, that require every bit of knowledge from our past. These are still issues from the days of the Silk Road and the Great Game that are playing out as we speak."

As Mr. Smith spoke, Li Jihua and two other men hurried into the room. When Smith had finished, they leaned down and whispered something urgently into his ear. After delivering their message, they stood silently behind the seated gentleman, whose bloodshot eye now showed signs of a twitch.

"Mark Jamison," Mr. Smith announced, "tonight you will see a cultural program instead of meeting our president."

"Did something happen?"

Li Jihua answered. "I received news just now that a 500-pound bomb was found where the president was to speak later today. Report says it fell off an army truck passing by. The visit has been cancelled."

"Uighur separatists?" Jamison asked.

The three men looked at each other, clearly not knowing how to respond.

CHAPTER

23

Mr. Smith asked the others to sit down. "Maybe Mr. Jamison deserves a real answer to his separatist question. Sir, kindly indulge me while I attempt to answer."

"Of course." Jamison had a feeling that his long journey to China would be worthwhile, after all.

"Please, take some more coffee as I begin."

The story Mr. Smith told was more informative than Jamison could have imagined.

"You will recall that the wealth of the Soviet Union was incredible, even if it did collapse from financial mismanagement. It contained the greatest amount of the world's resource wealth. Its reserves of oil and natural gas, gold, diamonds, and just about anything else you might care to think of were unsurpassed. When the breakup of the Soviet Union came in 1990, energy-rich areas like Azerbaijan, Kazakhstan, and Turkmenistan were set free as independent republics. The global race was immediately on to control their oil and natural gas reserves. Of course, Russia had the advantage of historical relationships and proximity, and many of the new republics were landlocked between Russia and China. Still, the West coveted their resources and looked for ways to both get them and deprive Russia of its historic control over them.

"What ensued was not so much a continuation of the Cold War as a new chapter of the old Great Game, the battle for Central Asia's resource wealth pitting the British squarely against Russia once again. Of course, this time the United States was a full partner of Britain. Have you heard of Shah Deniz and the Baku-Ceyhan pipeline?"

Jamison's face showed no recognition.

"How about *Nabucco*?"

Jamison had to work hard to suppress a flash of recognition.

"The West welcomed the new Russian Republic not with a Marshall Plan to help get it on its feet, but with plans to strip away the region's resources without offering any benefit to Russia. The pipelines I just named are a few of the new competing energy corridors, some of which are siphoning off the former Soviet Union's energy treasures and taking them to the West in pipelines that bypass Russia entirely. Caspian Sea oil is already flowing to Ceyhan in Turkey on a route that steers clear of Russia or Armenia and connects the Turkic countries. I don't have to tell you how long Turkey has been after these resources, and I don't have to tell you how long it has tried to erase Armenia from the map because it has been in Turkey's path eastward.

"Next, the West tried *Nabucco*, the most ambitious project to date, which would have carried Central Asian energy all the way to the heart of Europe—to Austria—for distribution, once again bypassing Russia entirely. Russia responded with its Nord Stream pipeline and Gazprom's proposed South Stream pipeline, both skirting around Ukraine to get Russian natural gas directly into Germany. Why bypass Ukraine? The West would tell you otherwise, but Russia sees Ukraine as a chokehold on its natural gas exports to Europe.

"Our own country now has a pipeline from Dubai that connects through our "oil city" refineries in Gwader, Baluchistan, which is part of Pakistan, as you know. The Chinese pipeline heads north from there along the Karakoram Highway and into China, terminating here in Urumqi. We are in the process of feeding the western end of our pipeline with Iraqi oil. We have also acquired our own oil and natural gas fields in Kazakhstan, and the Russians responded with the Power of Siberia pipeline, which allows them to sell directly here.

"I tell you all of this for a reason, Mr. Jamison: The energy corridors are the new Silk Road and a major part of the revised Great Game, which is every bit as dangerous as the old one. It is a very deadly game, in fact."

Jamison listened intently and continued to sip his coffee, thanking Mr. Smith for the information when the opportunity arose. "I want you to know how much I appreciate the background you are providing me, and I look forward to learning how this relates to the bomb that was discovered here today."

Mr. Smith acknowledged his thanks and continued. "Mr. Jamison, you certainly recall the near total destruction of your people by the Turks while the British helped them in a war against the Russians. I think you would not find it inappropriate if I said your ancient race, in its ancient homeland, became pawns on the chessboard of the Great Game. Well, I submit to you that the innocent Armenian families who fled to Syria during the Genocide are today being killed alongside innocent Syrian Arabs and Kurds for much the same reason as before.

"The British were in the forefront—along with Qatar, Saudi Arabia, Israel, France, and America—in stirring up the 'Day of Rage,' which clearly didn't proceed as intended. My sources confirm that the operation was run out of London. The British tried to get Assad to agree to a pipeline that would run Qatar's and the Saudi's natural gas through Syria and then into the Turkish pipeline to move the gas on to Europe, but Assad didn't want to cut Russia out of the picture. Instead, it agreed to another $10 billion deal that would take both Iran's and Iraq's natural gas to its own terminus and offer it to the European pipelines from there. The Iran-Iraq-Syria pipeline incensed Qatar and Saudi Arabia, who demanded Assad's removal from leadership.

"The object of Operation Day of Rage was to remove Assad from power in Syria because, as I said, he and the Russians sought to make Syria the terminus of a pipeline coming

from the largest repository of natural gas in the world—
Iran. Joining that pipeline would be Russia's South Stream
pipeline, bringing in Caspian oil and natural gas. We are
interested in the idea of this Syria-Russia pipeline project
and have not hidden our interest in or our need for Iranian
natural gas. Without the clean energy that natural gas pro-
vides, China's people are being asphyxiated by coal emis-
sions.

"Of course, Israel was happy to sign on to any plan that
would weaken Syria and Iran, so it joined this Operation
Day of Rage. Assad ran into a well-funded and coordinated
effort to unseat him through such efforts as using social
media, at which the West excels, and paying off Syrian officials and officers to defect, and so on.

"I don't have to tell you about the mess this created in
Syria. There have already been vastly more innocent casual-
ties there than Iraq experienced in the Gulf conflicts, at
least so far. When Syrians wouldn't defect from the Assad
regime, Qatar and the Saudis brought in hired guns from
outside, including al Qaeda and its affiliates. Because of this,
Turkey saw an opening to deal with the Kurds and secure
parts of oil-rich northern Iraq, but this is another matter for
another time.

"I believe your American company Bechmann Engineering knows all about this, as it was involved many years
ago in getting Iraq's Saddam Hussein to build a pipeline.
Saddam balked at a suggested terminus in Israel, agreeing
to Aqaba instead, but that wasn't good enough for the
American company, so the backers scuttled the deal and
began lobbying to scuttle Saddam and his Baath Party leadership. I realize that I am giving you a very lengthy answer to
your question, but I assure you that we are nearing the point
of it all."

"Please continue."

"So, the USA instead engaged in the TAPI pipeline in
Afghanistan, bringing natural gas from Turkmenistan to

India via Afghanistan and Pakistan, as a counterbalance to the Iran-Pakistan pipeline. The Taliban were employed by the Americans and British to protect one project and to harass construction of the other.

"As you can see, the new game has now spread across the entire Middle Eastern region, and the respective governments are so caught up in supporting their natural gas and oil services industries that it simply becomes hard for them to say no or to condition their level of support, even if it drags nations to war or violates all logic.

"Imagine, the UK and the USA are supporting the murderous Chechen rebels because their independence movement is within a part of Russia that affects the Caspian and potentially the resource movements from that region—let me repeat that: It is within Russia and those rebels are still receiving support from the West. The Russians continue the Nagorno Karabagh standoff to keep Armenia and Azerbaijan dependent on Moscow, and the recent moves with Ukraine and Crimea are seen by Russia as stemming from the same kind of Western intrusions that stirred up the mess in Syria after Assad. It sees the Ukraine as a potential block to its bid to reach the West, while the West looks at Russia's efforts only militarily and keeps them out of its European Union.

"Now, about that bomb found today—our sources reveal that the British and the Americans are funneling funds to Uighur causes that encourage the separatists. If the bomb was not an accident, and I doubt it was, it was likely a part of the new Great Game. It could have killed the president of the People's Republic of China today, maybe even taking you with him while you were shaking his hand. I ask you, Mr. Jamison, whether or not this entire new Great Game is totally out of control and vastly too risky to be continued."

"Based on what you just stated, it certainly appears to be."

Mr. Li spoke up. "This is why we want you to approach the new Pope. We know how persuasive you can be. We know you can help us get the Vatican and the Russians to agree to a way of ending this madness. If the Pope can bring the British, the Americans, and the other major players into this quest for peace, maybe there is a chance we can succeed."

Mr. Smith continued. "Mr. Jamison, in each case of manipulation of local interests for this game, calamity has resulted. A door gets opened, and a group like al Qaeda walks in and creates a disaster through insecurity and killing. There are no two countries more opposed to fundamentalist Muslim violence and separatism than Russia and China, which was why we created the Shanghai Council Accords. Russia will not surrender Chechnya to rebels, and China will never surrender any aspect of Xinjiang. We don't appreciate those who meddle in our internal affairs, no matter what the rubric employed may be, and we don't believe that the killing of innocents has anything to do with freedom of expression. The more the West stirs things up, the more it harms all of us. There will be less freedom for anyone, anywhere in the world, as well. As Mr. Li correctly pointed out, we think the involvement of the Pope will assist greatly in our efforts at resolving the Great Game."

"I don't know why you think I know the new Pope, but I will certainly do what I can to make your views known to those of goodwill whom I do know, who might make a difference."

Finally, the third person in the room, who was never introduced and who had remained silent to this point, spoke up in Chinese. Li Jihua translated. "Mr. Wei Tong believes that you need to find the secret you seek and use it to help resolve the differences that threaten us all. We all do," he added.

At this, Mr. Smith rose to his feet, followed by the others. "Even if the key was ours at one time, we do not ask for the return of the secret—only its employment, as Mr. Wei has requested."

As they shook hands, Mr. Wei had one final thought for Jamison: "Don't forget that the largest US producer and supplier of natural gas is British Petroleum. Look closely, and you will see its handprint on everything."

24

Li Jihua accompanied Mark Jamison on what Mark believed would be the ride back to his hotel. Jamison took the occasion to ask Li Jihua about Mr. Wei Tong and Mr. Smith.

"Mr. Smith works for Mr. Wei. Mr. Wei is a very important man; he may be the richest man in Xinjiang. He runs our largest industrial conglomerate, the Xinjiang D'Fray Group."

"Do you also work with the D'Fray Group, Mr. Li?"

"I work for Vice Governor Jun, who is the vice governor of Xinjiang. You will meet him now, before we go to the hotel. He will host you tonight for the cultural evening and a special dinner in your honor."

"Don't tell me, more *Gam Bays* tonight?"

"Very many more. You will have a great time. Vice Governor Jun is the best host in all of China!"

Mark swallowed hard and tried to close his eyes as the minivan raced along. At least the roads were well paved, he thought to himself. Then a question struck him.

"Why the vice governor and not the governor of Xinjiang?"

"The governor is Uighur. Vice Governor Jun makes the important decisions."

Mark fell back into slumber and came to when the minivan door swung open. Mr. Li walked Jamison inside a large, well-decorated residence with red-leather upholstered and dark stained furniture that looked neither Oriental nor European. Mark was invited to sit while attendants brought tea and trays of fresh fruit.

"The vice governor will see you when he finishes his meeting," Li announced.

Mark closed his eyes and dozed off again. The sound of voices behind the door became audible as those inside approached the end of their meeting. When an attendant opened the door, Jamison saw Malcolm Wyle standing beside a very tanned Victor Domich, who was shaking the hand of someone whom Mark assumed was Vice Governor Jun. Mark rose to his feet.

"Ah, Mark," Wyle exclaimed. "Victor, this is the gentleman I was speaking of, Mark Jamison. Mark, I don't know if you've met Victor before."

"I only know him by reputation and seeing him often on the news. It is a pleasure to meet you, sir."

Domich, in turn, introduced Jamison to Vice Governor Jun, referring to Jun as an old and dear friend and a partner with Bechmann Engineering in the economic development of the province.

Instead of leaving, Domich proceeded to lecture Jamison on the power of provincial leaders in China's decentralized system of governance. The vice governor offered Jamison a cigarette before lighting his own, perfectly content to let Domich speak.

Mark's introduction to the vice governor was brief, and he was escorted out with Wyle and Domich, who continued his lecture on provincial power as they walked. "The Muslim rebellion that proclaimed an independent Turkestan in Xinjiang in 1865 was led by Yakub Beg, an agent of the British, who sought to counter Russian influence here." Domich's point throughout his lecture was that when necessary, outside influence had a way of reaching anywhere— even this region, furthest from any body of water.

Mark thought of the Anglo-Xinjiang Alliance office he visited in London with Wyle and his meeting there with the strange Franz Gottlieb. Jamison said nothing, because he knew that Domich was determined to help his client and would use any means at his disposal to do so.

Li Jihua escorted Mark Jamison back into the minivan for the return to his hotel and his anxiously awaited afternoon nap before the evening's cultural presentation and dinner. On the drive back, Mr. Li argued continually with the driver, who was apparently an unfamiliar, unexpected replacement for the one who drove them about in the morning, while both men were speaking into their cell phones. Mark didn't know exactly where they were when the minivan abruptly veered off to the side of the road, but another van, immediately ahead of theirs, did the same. Jamison presumed the men who exited and approached them were security for guests of the vice governor, so he was baffled when they dragged him out of the minivan, threw tape over his mouth, bound his wrists together, and shoved him into their van.

He looked out the window in vain for Li Jihua, immediately becoming as frightened as he was exhausted when he didn't see him. The van was spun around, and Mark fell sideways, unable to catch himself. One of the men took advantage of his position and held him down and out of the view of passing traffic. Most of Mark's body was gathered on the floorboard while his head and arms were held against the seat beside the menacing fellow, who continued to push his head down.

Mark had never before felt so entirely out of control. He was angry with himself for ever coming to this place. He knew how dangerous it was. If these were Uighur rebels, his head would be considered detachable, and it would be a perfect gift for the vice governor, carrying the message that even his guests were vulnerable. If they ransomed Mark off as a hostage, he hoped Malcolm Wyle would persuade Victor Domich to help finance his release. He reviewed all the possibilities, deciding that the ride was about as miserable as the crowded plane he had been jammed into the previous night to get here. At least he was now spared the taste of unwashed hair. Still, his body jostled with every turn and bump on the hard floor, and he was damned scared, even though he told himself not to be.

He'd closed his eyes; he didn't know if he had fallen asleep. He was slow to remember all the things he was supposed to do and listen for if ever taken hostage, and he did none of them. He was unaware of how long he had been travelling, what turns were made, or what sounds he might have discerned along the way. All he was sure of was that any body of water was still a long way off.

He was pulled out of the van by two men, stood upright, and walked into a Quonset hut that seemed to be on an old airfield. He saw lots of oil-field equipment on the way into the hut, some of which was still in crates. He thought he heard voices speaking, but the language wasn't Chinese or any that he could decipher. They brought him inside and painfully removed the tape over his mouth, speaking the first words he'd heard since his kidnapping: "Alright, just sit down and keep your mouth shut."

These Chinese guys spoke perfect American English. Mark sat down in a chair the man indicated.

"Okay, okay. Where are you guys from?"

"I mean it. Quiet, or the tape goes back on."

"Okay, I understand." Jamison shut his mouth; he was thinking more clearly now. These weren't Uighur rebels by a long stretch. All of this was too neat.

I'll bet these fellows were trained by Langley, he thought. *Maybe even went to the Farm at Quantico…A false-flag snatch.* He knew the terminology and procedures of such an operation, but never thought he would be the target. He knew that even friendlies could be brutal during these operations, and didn't want to press his luck.

Instead, he pointed to his groin with a plaintive look in his eyes.

"Yeah, okay—first door over there."

Jamison stood up, stretched, and looked at his bound wrists, then at the man who spoke to him.

"You can manage," was the only reply he got.

He did so and returned to his seat. He heard a great deal of activity on the airstrip; trucks were being loaded and gear hauled off. He thought they were probably near the oil fields close to the Kazahkstan border, which would explain the language he'd heard, but didn't understand.

An airplane landed outside, something that sounded like either a small regional jet or a substantial executive jet. This time he heard voices outside speaking English, meaning that people from the aircraft were approaching the Quonset hut. His earlier suspicions of a false-flag operation were being confirmed, and he felt greatly relieved in knowing that he would most likely be keeping his head on his shoulders...Unless the false flag wanted to send a really strong message entirely at Mark's expense. He had never heard of anything that extreme being done before, though, so he quickly put this idea out of his mind...Mostly.

The door opened with animated conversation. His abductors said they needed to get back to Urumqi before they were missed, and the newly arrived gentleman thanked them and asked to have Mark's hands freed up before they left. Again, pulling the tape hurt, this time tearing a lot of hair from his arms, which was proof that he was half Armenian, even if his nose wasn't.

"Thanks, fellows," he couldn't resist calling out as his abductors left. Mark could finally see the gentleman standing in the doorway.

"Franz Gottlieb. Why am I not surprised to see you here?"

"Just relax, Jamison. You have some other friends coming to visit." Victor Domich and Malcolm Wyle appeared in the doorway as if on cue.

"Gentlemen, so much drama." Mark couldn't resist ribbing his captors again. "I would have invited you for a drink at my hotel if you asked…Of course, I'm not even sure which hotel that is. It's been kind of a whirlwind trip."

"It's the Ramada Plaza," Gottlieb responded, not rising to Mark's sarcasm.

"Thank you. Will I be returning there?"

"That depends."

"On?"

"What you tell us about your meeting this morning with Wei Tong."

"I didn't even know I had a meeting with him. He only said a few words to me."

"What words, exactly?"

"He wants the intrigue around here to stop, says it's getting too dangerous."

"Did he say anything about Bechmann?"

"Nothing. He said BP was behind everything."

With that, Domich and the others looked relieved. Domich asked for clarification. "So he focused on the British, then? Nothing about American companies?"

"Nothing at all. Why did you folks have me grabbed like this? To make it look like a Uighur rebel job, I assume."

"Just in case."

"In case what?"

"In case Wei comes after us and doesn't want to cooperate. Same with the vice governor."

"You mean that if they don't cooperate, you'll mess the place up a bit for Bechmann's sake."

"For all of our sakes…For America, for Christ's sake! You don't want the Russians around here, do you? It's bad enough that BP is all over the place."

"So what happens to me now, Victor?"

"That depends," Gottlieb answered.

"You said that before. I'm getting a little nervous about this, folks. You know I don't work for your law firm, Victor, or for Bechmann, or for anyone else messing around out here. Why me?"

"Maybe." Gottlieb seemed to be answering for all three of them.

"Maybe?! What the hell is that supposed to mean?" Mark now knew for certain that he had to convey Mr. Wei Tong's message to the Vatican. Wei was right; things have become too dangerous on this chessboard. Mark wanted to end the suffering these exact kinds of maneuvers had brought to the world. Wyle and Domich and Gottlieb, whoever he really was, were making their fortunes promoting the chaos. Mark was not on their side in this game. He was convinced now, more than ever, of which side he was on.

"Look, the engines are still running on your jet. I don't know where you're headed next, but get me out of here and I'll play whatever role you want. I'm not sure what you think I know, but I probably don't. Just get me out of here."

"Maybe." Gottlieb again spoke for all three of them.

Mark felt heavily the combination of lack of sleep, anger at the indignities being heaped upon him by these assholes, and anger at the centuries of global indifference to the plight of pawns on the chessboard welling up within him. It was time to act. Without thinking, he lunged at Victor Domich, grabbed his left arm, and spun him around in a hammerlock, Mark's right arm poised to break his neck.

"Now, let's get to the airplane and get out of here," Jamison commanded. Wyle was stunned; he waved Gottlieb off. Mark didn't think Wyle or Domich would be foolish enough to be carrying weapons, but Gottlieb might be. He had doubtlessly been trained to kill, in any event.

Jamison ordered Gottlieb and Wyle to go ahead of him and then lurched forward, Domich's head and slowly breaking arm and shoulder firmly in his grasp as he pushed the lawyer along.

"Ease up on my arm. I'm not a kid anymore, asshole."

"Just keep walking."

A female figure emerged from the open front door of the executive jet and hurried down its accommodation steps and toward the men. Mark recognized Carol Durlen as she got closer to them.

"Victor, are you alright? What's going on?"

"Just get back in the plane. It looks like we picked up another passenger."

"Mark, is that you?"

"Looks like I'm going to get another free ride from you, Carol."

"What the—" Victor began to mumble, wincing in pain as he marched forward in Mark's hammerlock, his head pulled far to its side.

"When your passengers are seated with belts on and this plane starts its taxi, I'll release Victor and we'll all enjoy a smooth flight," Mark promised his pilot friend.

"Victor?" Carol asked, wanting to confirm their itinerary.

"Moscow as planned. Nothing's changed. And bring this asshole a bottle of scotch to relax him—my shoulder is damn near broken."

Carol's copilot brought everything needed for drinks to all the passengers, and their taxi commenced. Mark released Victor and both men sat down, belted in, and poured themselves generous drinks.

Mark never heard Gottlieb unfasten his belt or slide up behind him, but he felt the explosion in his head and dropped his full glass as Gottlieb knocked him out with one punch to his temple.

At least Jamison was able to sleep on this flight.

25

Moscow

When Mark Jamison came to, he felt grateful for the punch. It seemed to have quieted the hostility among the passengers and given the pilot a good dose of loving sympathy for him—she was afraid they killed him. Mark could tell that her shows of concern for him left Victor Domich steaming, though he tried hard to conceal it. Mark asked Carol to bend low over him and didn't hide his whispers of affection.

Carol was beginning to realize that Mark was different than her other passengers, despite his strong-armed entry aboard the plane. She knew that people like Victor Domich hid a ruthless side beneath their veneers of polished success; that they got their way no matter the consequences to others. Mark seemed to be totally opposite that; she saw this groggy, half beaten-up fellow as very vulnerable.

During the flight, Mark felt confident enough in Carol to slip her a message asking her to radio a message to the Vatican informing Archbishop Scheuer of Mark's scheduled arrival in Moscow and requesting his help with contacts at the Kremlin. He also wanted her to convey that he had news from China that would interest the new Pope. Since she knew their hotel arrangements in Moscow, she could add that information. He asked her to destroy the message once she sent it, which she did.

The throbbing in Mark's temple and across his forehead continued throughout the flight. They arrived in Moscow and were greeted by a low-level staff member from

Domich&Carey's Moscow office who arranged arrival matters. The party was whisked into a waiting limousine that took them to the Ritz-Carlton, very near to the southern end of Red Square. The front of the old hotel looked up to nearby St. Basil's and across to the Kremlin. Mark had stayed there in the old Brezhnev days and was pleased with Victor's choice. He was also pleased that Victor offered everyone a drink at the old bar while those with bags had them taken to their rooms. A recollection of earlier days came to Mark's mind, which he mentioned, and Victor kindly said they would be interested in hearing it. Mark thought he'd even caught a glimpse of a smile on Domich's face, which relieved him considerably.

Mark's story started in the same bar thirty years earlier. It had been nearing midnight on a warm summer night when he'd decided to watch the change in shifts of the old Soviet guards in front of Spasky Tower. He found the precision of their movements extraordinary, and Moscow was incredibly quiet in those days. He stood by the Spasky Gate and surveyed the scene at Red Square. Other than the guards on duty, he was the only figure in the entire square at that time of night. Then he noticed a solitary figure slowly walking toward him from the far north end; it seemed to be deliberately heading directly for him. Mark stood there without turning his head, but watched from the corner of his eyes as the figure continued to approach steadily and directly toward him. Finally, a man stood literally shoulder to shoulder with him, practically touching him.

The scene must have looked like a classic meeting from an old spy novel, though nothing had been arranged. The individual was standing so close to Mark that his hand twitched in anticipation of a message being stuffed into it. Neither of them said anything. Finally, Mark took a deep breath and turned his head to look at the face of the gentleman. It was someone he instantly recognized and greeted by name—the well-known film star Kirk Douglas. Jamison blew out a sigh of relief as they began chatting about his movies and life back in California. Douglas had directed a film that was being shown at a festival there and was staying at the same hotel, which was then called simply the Hotel Moscow, Mark recalled. They'd strolled back together and had an enjoyable drink in the same part of the bar now occupied by Jamison, Domich, Wyle, Gottlieb, and the still very lovely Carol Durlen.

The group seemed to like the story. Domich volunteered to host a late dinner, which they all enjoyed. During dinner, Mark finally got the courage to ask about plans for the following day. The other men looked at each other, not disclosing their plans or what they might have in store for Jamison. Carol looked down to avoid seeing Mark's obvious discomfort. He was convinced that they were going to come at him again for information, but not knowing how this would be done or whose services would be engaged for this purpose was very unsettling to him.

To break the quiet after Mark's question, Domich promised that he would arrange to have Mark's suitcase sent to Moscow from Urumqi and would let everyone know that the very resourceful Mr. Jamison had safely escaped from an obvious Uighur kidnapping attempt. Domich also suggested that Jamison arrange a room for himself in the hotel on Domich's dime, which Mark did following dinner when the others headed up to their rooms.

Mark took the lowest priced room he could get, which wasn't much considering its huge price tag. He understood that Domich's generosity was obviously curbed by his sore shoulder and neck, just as Mark's head still ached from the sucker punch delivered to him on the jet, but he appreciated the room. Finally, after a long, hot shower, Mark was going to get a real sleep in a comfortable bed. He had just pulled back the covers when he heard a timid knock on his door. When he answered it, Carol Durlen stood before him, asking if he was alright.

Motioning for her to come inside, he tried to answer her. "I'm not sure at all what went on today, but I think you saved me for a second time."

"You mean Nairobi?"

"And now Urumqi."

"Well, maybe you saved me too. Victor can be a pretty forceful guy."

"You mean you two aren't a couple?"

"He does try, but I have my own room, if that's what you mean."

Mark put his arms around her and stared into those large green eyes. "You know, getting you off my mind has been one of the toughest things I've had to do."

"Yeah, well, getting smacked in the head by Franz had to be right up there, also. You were out for over an hour. I was really scared, and I think Franz was, too. He didn't want to kill you, after all. Malcolm and Victor were beside themselves with anger toward him."

"I'm fine. I see three of you now, but that's not so bad…It's a lovely thought, really."

"Please don't joke about all of this."

"Well, I'm not sure what I'm supposed to be doing. Did you get the message off to the Vatican?"

"As instructed, sir."

"Gee, I like the sound of that. Did any message come back?"

"Just an acknowledgement of receipt of the message."

"Thank you." He brushed his lips gently over hers, and she closed her eyes.

A knock on the door at that moment was loud and hard, interrupting their kiss, and the timing was sure unfortunate. When he opened it, two uniformed policemen pushed their way inside the room.

"You are Mark Jamison? Identification."

He reached for his wallet, which he was lucky to have on him, and showed them what they wanted to see.

"Who is this woman?"

"An old friend."

"Not your wife?"

"No." His betrayal of Sarah stuck into him like a knife blade in his side. He looked at Carol, and she cast her eyes down.

"Put on your clothes. You must come with us."

"Can't I stay here until morning? I haven't had a real sleep in a long time."

"Sorry. Get dressed."

Mark looked down and realized that he was wearing only his boxers and an undershirt. "I'm so sorry, Carol."

"Hurry," the policeman said. "We are to take you elsewhere. You can sleep there."

"One moment please."

He looked Carol in the eyes and breathed deeply of her scent. "What's meant to be and what's not meant to be," he whispered. Out loud, he said, "You'd better get to your room and enjoy a sleep for both of us." He gave her a kiss, but her eyes were wide open this time.

The police escorted Jamison to their marked car, which was immediately in front of the hotel. Its orange flashers were throwing a bizarre pattern of light into the very dark night.

"Where are you taking me?"

"To a nicer apartment."

"Better than the Ritz-Carlton?"

"You'll see."

They spoke on mobile phones as they drove only a short distance away, entering the large Kremlim compound from a gated side street just off Red Square. From there, they proceeded slowly and twisted through narrow lanes until they reached a palatial residence on the grounds that Mark learned was now used as apartments for visitors of the president of Russia.

"You are now a guest of President Putin. Your wing is number four. Good night."

The residence looked like part of the Hermitage Museum—the decorations were ornate and historic. He found his way to his wing in the subdued lighting. As he opened the door, he immediately thought of Carol, and then of Sarah. Maybe the police had come at the right time, after all. In the main bedroom, a huge bed beckoned.

Just as he'd pulled his shoes off, he heard the doorbell chime. He found some slippers in the bedroom closet and padded his way through seven rooms to the front door of his apartment.

"Yes?"

"Mr. Jamison, my name is Constantine Popov. I am the personal assistant of President Putin, who sends his warm greetings. I extend my warm greetings to you, also." Popov embraced him and kissed him on both cheeks.

Mark found himself slightly flustered. "I didn't know you folks still did that here."

"I only pass along the greetings directed by our president. He looks forward to seeing you personally in the morning, and I will be by for you at ten o'clock. Your breakfast cart will arrive at nine. Is there anything you wish in the meantime?"

"Just an answer to one question: Did the Vatican arrange this?"

"Of course. You and I seem to be working with the same contact there: Archbishop Scheuer, the assistant to former Cardinal Ratzinger, now Pope Benedict."

"One more thing, please—could someone notify the Ritz-Carlton to cancel my room?"

"It's already taken care of, and there will be no charge. Also, Victor Domich has been informed that you are under the personal protection of the president. Since he maintains an office here and derives a great deal of income from his

Russian clients, I am certain you will hear nothing further from him or the others in his party. You have nothing more to concern yourself with in regard to them. If there is nothing else, I will plan to see you again in the morning. Sleep well."

Mark did.

CHAPTER

26

The morning bell rang in his suite ahead of schedule, and he didn't know who or what it might be. He suppressed thoughts of Carol Durlen standing in a nightgown and waiting for him on the other side of the door.

He opened it to find only an old suitcase sitting in front of his door. Suspicious of the case, Jamison took it slowly inside and carefully opened it, finding clothing and not a bomb. Amidst the odd assortment of clothing was a note handwritten on presidential stationery. Jamison picked up the note and read the following:

Welcome, Mark. We took up a collection of clothes for you upon news of your arrival, just like you and your staff did for me in Salzburg when my suitcase didn't arrive with my flight.

It was signed simply, *Vlad*.

Mark tossed his head back and laughed. How could a man with Putin's schedule have time for this? How could anyone in his position be so thoughtful? *Or funny*, he thought as he pulled out bizarre items of clothing, some in sizes too small and some being women's undergarments in sizes vastly larger than anything he ever hoped to see worn.

He left the bag by the door and showered before his breakfast cart arrived. He heard the next ring at his door while drying himself off. Again he padded his way through the various ornate rooms to his door. This time there was a clothes rack on wheels holding a black suit in his size and a number of shirts and neckties. Beside it was a pigskin suitcase that was neatly packed with underclothes, sweaters, and a shaving kit.

There was no note with this set of clothes, and there didn't need to be. Mark gratefully took everything to his bedroom and put it all to good use. He was fully shaved and dressed when the cart arrived at nine with a chef to prepare his omelet and pour his juice and coffee. Jamison was enjoying the once-neatly folded *International Herald Tribune* and a second cup of coffee when Constantine Popov arrived precisely on time for the schedule he'd indicated last night.

"Well, how did you sleep, Mark?"

"Like a man who has come in from the cold."

"I take it that means you had a good rest?"

"Yes, it was one that was fully appreciated."

"And the clothing fits okay?"

Mark stood and did a 360-degree turn for Popov's sartorial inspection.

"It's a good fit, and it becomes you. Will you be ready in half an hour to meet with the president? It will need to be very brief due to his established schedule today, but he has expressed great pleasure in getting a chance to see you again."

Jamison made a final scan of the newspaper, dismayed at the news of the world, and couldn't help but make a comment. "Constantine, the world seems to be spiraling out of control…This has to change."

Popov looked solemnly at Mark. "Our president sees it the same way. That is another, more important reason that he wants to meet with you today."

"And I him, Constantine. And I him." Mark motioned for Constantine to lead the way.

"Is walking okay?" Popov asked.

"Sure."

They headed out and walked through a labyrinth of narrow lanes to get to a major lane through the Kremlin being used by briefcase-carrying young men and women who were scurrying about to their various ministry meetings. The scene seemed interchangeable with any one of those he had observed in Washington, London, Madrid, or Paris. Perhaps the closest comparison was with Rome, he thought. Maybe there was something to the notion of Russia being the Third Rome.

There were steps and more steps—people in the Kremlin kept fit. There were doors and badges and all the things he was used to back in Washington, but there was a difference. The young women seemed to notice him here, looking at him as they did back at the US State Department thirty years before. In this time span, the women stateside seemed to have steadily lost the feminine charms that made working alongside them so pleasant, even inspiring at times. The Russian women were always thought in the West to be more masculine and insensitive, but he wasn't seeing that. *What a role reversal,* he thought as he acknowledged the nods of heads, winks of eyes, and flirtatious expressions as Constantine passed with his American accompaniment. The care with which these women presented themselves, even if they were just modern file clerks, reminded Jamison of Hollywood starlets.

"Can you get me a job here, Constantine?" Mark half joked.

Popov smiled. "I know what you mean. I look forward to coming to work here—I'm married with two kids, but this keeps me going." Popov opened a door and ushered Mark inside it. "This is the outer office, where we'll sit for a moment until called." As Mark sat and waited, Popov received messages from staff and signed off on various reports. "We work hard around here, Mark, just to keep our little world from 'spinning out of control'—I like your phrase."

In a few minutes, the president emerged with a number of young staff gathered around him, yellow pads or laptops in hand. He was speaking in Russian and looked to be thanking them for getting on their assignments, which were all probably due within a few hours, just as in the White House.

He turned to focus on Jamison. "Mark, you are here! Welcome. Come in, come in."

Popov followed Mark inside and watched as his boss gave Mark the same greeting Popov had been asked to convey the previous night. "Sit down, sit down," Putin requested. Mark and Constantine complied. Mark beamed at seeing this former vice rector now one of the most important figures on the planet.

Before he could begin to speak, Putin asked him about Sarah and the children. Mark told him they were all doing well and explained how proud his family had been learning of his rise to the presidency.

To add some levity, he added, "Of course, we knew it was your time with us at the Global Forum that got you to the top back here in Moscow."

"Of course, it didn't hurt," Putin joked. "Tell me about that son of yours. He really impressed me, you know."

"He's just joined the Navy. He wants to be a naval attaché here in Russia before long. Somehow, I think you will both reconnect, just as we are doing now." Mark ran his hands down the sides of his suit coat and complimented the president and his assistant on taking such great care of him, including his new attire. "If I had known in Salzburg what lay in store for you, we would have come up with better things for you during your stay there. Maybe even fresh-squeezed orange juice." It was an inside joke from the session they'd shared that brought a chuckle from the president.

Mark pulled the small purple pouch from his pocket, pulled out the gold coin, and handed it to Vladimir Putin. "I'll bet you remember this. I keep it with me always."

"Heraclius playing Byzantine chess and Pope John IV on the reverse. Of course! I was hoping it had aroused your curiosity. Since you reached out to us yesterday through our mutual friends in the Vatican, I assumed it had. To tell the truth, I also knew you had been showing the coin around, so

I didn't need to drop you another clue."

Jamison summarized what he'd learned about Heraclius and his efforts to spread Christianity, end the schism in the Christian church, and even his efforts with Muhammed to bring peace and a center to monotheism. "He did all this as emperor of the Roman Empire, the Second Rome. There are some who say that you want to make Russia the seat of the Third Rome."

"Mark, Russia doesn't need to be the center of anything, but there needs to be an established center. Across the globe, the churches are weak, the culture is weakening, and the forces of laissez-faire capitalism and resurgent nationalism are threatening. I would venture that unbridled and unscrupulous Western business interests and their continuation of the Great Game are sowing much of the chaos that the Islamists are feeding upon, and both are incredibly destructive. It looks to us as if the West is continuing to isolate Russia. When we freed ourselves from the Soviet system, instead of getting a Marshall Plan, we got a raid on our resources, our allies, and even our identity."

Jamison couldn't argue. "I remember that at the time of our Forum session, Yeltsin's folks were complaining that they were giving everything to the West and getting nothing in return. They warned that they would have to steer a less favorable course, being forced to do it to gain some bargaining leverage with the West."

"I also remember that, of course. I worked with him through those times," Putin responded. "Our nations should both be much further along than we are now, not bogged down with Great Game adventurism."

"What do you think about the Byzantine secrets of the *Liberia*? Some people suggested that you believe Ivan the Terrible hid things in tunnels under where we are sitting."

"Of course that's nonsense," Putin answered earnestly. "You are Armenian, and you know how Armenia has survived all these years. Your people are the smartest around—

if there was knowledge secreted away, it was secreted away by the Armenians. This is why I had the coin prepared showing Heraclius playing Byzantine chess. Everything from the old Silk Road came through Armenia, and everything from Persia or India also passed through Armenia. Chess decided the outcome of many disputes and conflicts in that time. Armenia has survived longer than any other nation. Think about it: Even with the deliberate annihilation of all Armenians by the Turks, your people are still here, with their own nation on their own soil...Or at least on a portion of it.

"We both know about the role of your friend, the Game Master Hani Waladoon. He has helped resolve intractable problems and remained hidden far behind the scenes. Use him again, and arm him with any secrets you may find. I will support you and him in every way possible. The Great Game must end. Russia can no longer tolerate its isolation from the West, and the Orthodox Church must be respected and once again integrated fully with the Church in Rome. Do these seem like things you can be helpful with? They are not for the sake of Russia alone, but for everyone's sake."

Putin turned to Popov and continued in Russian. Mark discerned that he was asking Popov to work with Jamison. Did he find him as worthwhile as the president did? Was his history of impetuousness troubling or an asset they could exploit? To each question, Popov responded that he could work with Jamison and already considered him a valuable person. He also reminded the president of how highly the Vatican thought of him and that the opinion of the Vatican would be critical to everything they were seeking to achieve.

Putin once again turned to Jamison and smiled, rising to his feet. Jamison and Popov did the same. "So Mark, I want you and Popov to work together to accomplish what we have been discussing. Find any secrets, share them with Hani, and work with the Vatican—after all, our guy is now the Pope. This is the time to act!"

As they walked toward the door, the president put his arm around Mark and asked him where he thought the secret strategies might be hidden.

Mark's response was simple and straightforward: "Where neither you nor the Vatican's Entity can get to them...But I think Hani and I will be able to. Trust us."

"I trust you, Mark Jamison." With that, the president gave Mark another hug and kiss on both cheeks. "Tell Sarah and the children I asked after them. Tell your son that he is welcome as the American attaché or ambassador at any time. I'll leave it to you and him to work on the Washington side of that posting."

"Thank you for this time together, Mr. President, and for your confidence and friendship."

"I am always Vlad to you, Mark. Keep close through Constantine, and best of luck."

Nagorno Karabagh

Before departing Moscow, Jamison formulated a plan
that would include Sarah. He would arrange to take her for
an extended vacation to Venice, and from there they would
make excursions to San Lazaro in order to develop relationships of sufficient confidence with the monastic community leaders. While there, they would inquire about its
archives and do what research they could. He and Sarah
would also find the chess players among the monks and
sound out what they might know about strategies from
materials that could be safeguarded on the island. If any
monks played Byzantine chess at the monastery, so much
the better, Mark thought.

Mark's plan was to befriend the most avid chess players
in San Lazaro and see who might be the most inquisitive and
the most cooperative. He could then introduce Hani to play
a few games with those people and see what they knew while
Mark started to uncover and drill down on anything in their
archives related to gaming strategies or anything else that
could assist him in his quest. Hani could spend as much
time there as he felt would be productive. At the very least,
the monks would all become better chess players and perhaps more informed about the treasures Mark was confident they were safeguarding. Mark would contact
Constantine Popov to set up a bank account with a financial
institution accepted in Venice, as well as a line of credit sufficient for Hani's needs.

Before launching this endeavor, there would need to be one stop. Mark had been invited to be an election monitor in the newly independent republic of Nagorno Karabagh, and he felt strongly that he and Sarah should do this together. If she agreed, they would begin their adventure there before heading to the more comfortable environs of the Veneto.

Jamison delayed his departure from Moscow for a few days because he found it remarkable to stay at the Kremlin under the care of the president. Two things motivated him to leave sooner rather than later, however: First, he didn't want to overstay his welcome in the presidential visitor suite. Second, he was determined to resist the temptation of contacting Carol Durlen and seeing her again before he left. The latter was resolved by compromising with himself and calling the Ritz-Carlton to check on her. Ms. Durlen was no longer staying there, he was informed. He was greatly relieved.

With that out of the way, he could focus more clearly on helping the deserving people of Karabagh and rebuilding his relationship with Sarah while saving the world. This was a combination he found worthy of his time, so shortly after his call to the Ritz-Carlton, he phoned Constantine Popov to secure air arrangements for him to get back to Sarah and, if the presidential office was amenable, to provide passage from California for both him and Sarah to Yerevan, where they would transfer to Karabagh and then, ten days later, proceed to Venice.

Mark assumed this would take some little while to clear with the appropriate authorities, but Constantine informed him that the tickets would be arranged within a few hours and awaiting him electronically that evening at the Aeroflot counter at Sheremetyevo International. Popov's next statement amazed Mark, because he hadn't relayed his plan to Putin's assistant, but Popov stated that a line of credit would be arranged that very day in the HSBC bank in Moscow that could be drawn upon in Yerevan or Venice. Finally, Popov said he had a business-class seat departing Moscow for Los Angeles at 9:20 that evening with a connection to San Francisco. Mark thanked him. As he put down the receiver, he realized that this was indeed the president's personal assistant.

Back home with Sarah, his news and plans were well received and the arrangements agreeable. In fact, Sarah looked forward to Yerevan and Karabagh far more than Venice; she was familiar with the latter, but had never accompanied Mark to Armenia and had always wanted to. There were a few days to prepare for the trip. Mark was getting reports of Azeri snipers shooting indiscriminately across the border, sometimes hitting young families living in Karabagh and blocking any use of its airport. The Azeri press also tried to intimidate the election monitors by reporting that its government threatened to use snipers to target polling places.

Mark decided to share everything with his wife and partner on this mission. Sarah took it upon herself, through her university contacts, to become fully conversant in all requirements for the acceptable international standards for elections and vote processing. Along with voting officials and academics from the University of California, they would be a part of one of the OSCE (Organization for Security and Cooperation in Europe) international monitoring teams who were coming from all major Western countries. As he became conversant himself with these requirements, Mark was surprised to learn that USA elections were also monitored by OSCE teams from around the world.

The initiation of the trip to the region was uneventful. Arriving in Yerevan, their OSCE team had to travel for a full day over narrow, winding mountain roads into an area that was as mountainous and beautiful as it was isolated. On the day of the elections, they traveled to many villages across the expanse of the tiny nation and saw the incredible seriousness of purpose and diligence not only of voting officials, but of every single person casting a vote. These were people who had lived not only under the old Soviet system, but who had been administered by the Turkic Muslim Azeris, who showed no love or appreciation for this ancient Christian people in its historic homeland. Upon the breakup of the Soviet Union, while other republics were granted their independence, the Karabagh Armenians who voted in this first election were instead attacked, forcing them to fight for their freedom. Both Mark and Sarah found the entire voting and counting procedure to exceed all standards and to be a very moving experience.

Election monitors from across the world agreed with their assessment. They also seemed emotionally moved at seeing the old and infirm turn out with a determination and pride that comes from the high price all there had paid for their freedom. Following the conclusion of all proceedings, Mark and Sarah joined all the teams heading back to Yerevan over the narrow winding road on another full day's journey.

In the following days, the Azeri Foreign Minister declared every election monitor to be Persona Non Grata, or PNG, and henceforth barred from ever entering Azerbaijan. Since Azerbaijan had never known a free election, it was unlikely that the nation would ever need election monitors. While Azerbaijan didn't have free elections, it did have plenty of something else—oil and natural gas. And so it went.

Sarah had accomplished what she had set out to do— she became an authority on free elections and their monitoring. She also became PNG in Azerbaijan, which both Sarah and Mark considered a high distinction. They joked that this status was suitable for rewarding with a special medal that one could wear to parties and receptions.

From Yerevan, they headed to Venice, where no one threatened to shoot them…At least, not upon their arrival or during their first day.

28

Venice

Mark's plan regarding San Lazaro was proceeding well. Their first visit to the Armenian Mekhitarist fathers had been preceded by a call from the Armenian Catholic Prelate in Vienna, arranged by Archbishop Atemian. This put Mark and Sarah directly in touch with San Lazaro's director, Father Mesrob, and set them up for a warm reception on their initial arrival to the island.

They toured the facilities, including the rooms in which Lord Byron lived while learning the Armenian language and writing that he was convinced it was the language employed by the Deity itself. The repositories and hermetically sealed vaults were discussed on the tour, and some were shown.

At one time, every Armenian publication had been collected by the fathers at San Lazaro. Today, the number of publications is too vast, which is certainly a positive development in the history of a people nearly annihilated and now growing in numbers and literary achievement around the world. When asked how far back the archives went on this tour, Mark was told they went as far back as the records of the nation and the people. Coins, currency, documents, and correspondence extended even to those items transmitted along the old Silk Road—some even earlier.

By the third visit, Mark and Sarah were introduced to Father Ishkan, a slight man with a dark complexion and a short-cropped beard whose skin glistened with perspiration.

He presented a noticeably moist palm when they shook hands. Father Ishkan came to the order from Syria and was reputed to be the chess champion of the group. Upon Mark's questioning, he indicated that he was learning Byzantine chess, but that he had no detailed or special knowledge of it. The father indicated that he would be interested in anything that was uncovered on the subject, but that there were others better able to research the collections, including young Deacon David from Massachusetts.

Deacon David turned out to be from Boston and a graduate of MIT. This young clergyman was also anxious to discover the treasures that he knew lay within the protected recesses of San Lazaro and used its system of computer files to check the references for various categories of materials. It was this young deacon who identified a file for Chinese documents dating back to the fifth century. Some were translated, and some were simply stored. There were also gifts that had been transmitted along the caravan routes and folios related to relations with the Persians and Byzantines.

Could something have been intended for a pope in Rome that didn't get passed along for some reason? "A definite possibility," was the deacon's reaction. "The popes were not popular with the Byzantines, or anybody else, back then."

Mark then asked the young man if he played any board games.

"Electronic versions, mostly."

"Did you study any gaming theory at MIT, anything that might have been based on the old board games like chess or its variations?"

"You mean like Byzantine chess?"

"What do you know about that?" Mark was surprised to find this opening so easily.

"It was the big thing on campus when I was there. There is a lot to the game—it's very complex."

"Do you think there might be something in these archives that relates to it? Maybe something that goes back to the days of Emperor Heraclius?"

"Give me some time, and I'll see what I can locate. I will need to run anything I find past Father Mesrob before I can share it with you, of course."

"That's fine. Is there anyone else here who might know about this sort of thing?"

"Father Ishkan is working on a book about ancient game variations. He's a master of Byzantine chess, and he's been doing research here for years."

"Thank you, David." That certainly didn't jibe with what Ishkan had told Mark, but it might explain his nervousness during their meeting. "How long has Father Ishkan been engaged in this project?"

"I've only been here six months, so I don't know. He's been here for close to seven years. I'm told he keeps mostly to himself outside of his games of chess."

"Do you know what his responsibilities are here in the order?"

"He speaks excellent Italian and is frequently the liaison if there are problems with local authorities. He also operates the order's boat, which the fathers often use for supplies and visits ashore. I tend to use the local vaporeto service, especially because it allows me to see the tourists and overhear their conversations. We get discounted fares and are sometimes treated like celebrities."

The next day, Mark and Sarah enjoyed a leisurely breakfast together in Venice. As they watched the activity along the canals come to life, Sarah suggested that shopping was a higher priority for her that day, so she would remain at their hotel while Mark returned to the island. Before leaving, he decided to contact Constantine Popov to see if he could track down Hani Waladoon. Mark asked Popov to relate that he had found something that would interest Hani and that he should contact Mark by mobile phone or at his hotel, the Ambassador Tre Rose, on a canal near San Marco Square.

Jamison anticipated that it would take days to track down a figure as mysterious as Hani. Popov phoned back within a half hour to say he'd been located in Beirut, working on resolving differences that had kept the West Bank and Gaza from cooperating. Popov said that Hani was working with both Hamas and Hezbollah factions on a game resolution to matters which needed to be resolved prior to an important series of United Nations votes. Hani said he would make every effort to be where Mark Jamison requested him to be at the earliest time possible. After this conversation, Mark phoned Father Mesrob to see if he might arrange another meeting with Father Ishkan. The meeting was arranged for two that afternoon.

Mark and Sarah continued their morning shopping together and tasted some local treats along the way. At 1:00 p.m., she walked him to the vaporeto landing and said she would continue looking at the various shops and museums until later in the afternoon and that her mobile phone would be on if he needed to reach her.

At the afternoon meeting, Father Ishkan continued to be guarded. He did agree to play a game of Byzantine chess with Mark's friend, who would soon be visiting the island. In the meanwhile, Mark wanted to probe Father Ishkan further on his knowledge of chess and board games. He asked if Ishkan had any thoughts on the origins of the game or of any other games he may have identified in the various collections during the course of his research. Again, Ishkan responded negatively. Did he know how far back the game went or of any special strategies associated with it? Father Ishkan did not share the research he had been conducting and compiling into his own book.

While they were meeting, Deacon David appeared at the door with his laptop. "I think I found a few things that will interest both of you."

Mark looked at Father Ishkan, who invited the deacon to sit down between them and open his screen.

"So, when Mr. Jamison asked me to look at our holdings related to Heraclius, a great deal turned up. He was in communication with the Tang Dynasty across the old Silk Road, which of course ended at their capital of Chang'an, today's Xi'an, which was the most populous and advanced city in the world at the time. He maintained these communications during what was the golden age of China's cosmopolitan culture. When Heraclius defeated the Persians at Ninevah, he reclaimed the True Cross and returned it to Jerusalem because the Persian king, Khosrau, traded every treasure he had to spare his life. The Tang Dynasty was pleased with the commercial and cultural exchanges with Heraclius and was delighted with his conquests. Armenian-born Heraclius was literally astride the crossroads of history, corresponding with the popes in Rome, the Chinese emperor, the defeated Persian emperor, and the newest figure to captivate everyone—Muhammed. Muhammed's followers were riding out of the dessert and spreading Islam at lightning speed. When Muhammed's followers conquered Persia, Persian Prince Pirooz fled to Tang China. The world was connected, and Heraclius was at its center.

"He wanted to unite the world in a peaceful fashion through a common Christianity that was supported by successful commercial interests and would set the stage for similar efforts that followed. Our holdings show references to a unique circular chess set that was packaged with accompanying Persian language books in a heavily jeweled case.

"Were they presented to Heraclius in Ninevah by the defeated King Khosrau, or did they find their way first as a tribute to the Tangs and then return along the old Silk Road as a gift of the Chinese to honor Heraclius? I couldn't find that answer."

Mark and Deacon David focused their eyes on Father Ishkan, who squirmed a bit and appeared to be perspiring profusely.

Deacon David continued. "Now we come to the really interesting part: The archive has been breached. I had to report to Father Mesrop on my way over here, and he said I could share this information with you. The security systems here stopped anything from leaving the premises, but there was a crude attempt to delete the holdings, probably as a first step to their removal."

Jamison asked about the value of those holdings.

"There is no value. They are beyond any conceivable valuation," the young deacon responded.

Father Ishkan was now visibly upset and trembling. "I wasn't going to go through with it," he wailed, "but I didn't know how to stop them! All I wanted was to understand the legacy, not to see it removed."

"Removed by whom? Who is after this?" Jamison inquired.

"Collectors, museum people—they come as tourists and offer the temptations of Satan. Father Mesrop and all who came before him are saints for preserving and protecting our history and the legacy of our people. I am not so strong, but I thank God for this meeting, because now they will never get so much as a coin or envelope from here. I will do anything to thwart them now."

Deacon David stood, saying he had better bring Father Mesrop over to join them right away, and left the room. Father Ishkan sat with his head in his hands, weeping. "I will never let them have anything. God grant me the strength to deal with what I have done."

They sat together for a few minutes, Ishkan crying silently, until the door opened and Father Mesrop and Deacon David came in.

"What arrangements have you made, and with whom have you made them?" Father Mesrop inquired of Ishkan.

He could be very direct when he sat down thanks to a quick hallway briefing from Deacon David.

"The collectors wouldn't take no for an answer! They preyed on my weakness. They knew my family was in Aleppo, and that our people there are starving again and far worse. My mother could never afford to see a doctor before, and now there are no doctors left alive."

"Has anything left the sanctuary or archives?"

"No, Father, I swear it—and nothing will."

"Who were these people, and what did you arrange? Is anyone else in the order involved? Be specific, or I can't be responsible for what happens to you." Father Mesrob was as stern as he could be.

"Father, I acted alone. I've taken nothing from them. They arranged a transfer for tomorrow evening, but it won't take place, I promise you. I swear it on my family."

"Who are they, Father Ishkan?" Mesrop pressed.

"A woman and gentleman. They came here claiming to be collectors for the British Museum. They were a very respectable older couple."

"Can you remember their names?"

"They said they were the Russells."

"That's the street the Museum is on! Great Russell Street!" Mark blurted out.

Father Mesrop shot a look toward Jamison that said, "One more word from you and you'll be escorted off the island." Jamison took the hint.

"Now, describe these people."

"She had light brown hair and large green eyes. He was very formal, wore an expensive suit, and spoke with an American accent. She was British. I overheard them talking about arriving from Moscow, but I think they had also been in China."

Mark choked back their identities and remained painfully silent.

"What is the plan for tomorrow evening?" Father Mesrop demanded.

"At six o'clock, I am to take our boat across to the Lido. It is to have motor problems and stop in the water until a small seaplane lands. I am to rendezvous with it. The door will open, and we will exchange briefcases. I am to have the jeweled Byzantine chess set and the books of Heraclitus, and they are to have $20 million in Euros and gold, silver, and platinum certificates."

"What happens next?"

"They depart by air, and I go on to the Lido, where the money will be deposited and as much will be transferred as needed for my family in Syria."

"Who is to meet you at the Lido?"

"My brother, Setrak—I didn't know what else to do or who to contact. Father, I am so ashamed. Please try to find it in your heart to forgive me."

"Forgiveness will come later. For now, we must plan a course of action. I want you to say nothing further of this to anyone. Be prepared to deliver yourself and a briefcase at the correct time and location so that these people can be caught by the authorities. Are you willing to do that?"

"Anything you direct."

"Deacon David, I would like you to prepare a tightly wrapped package with the weight you would ascribe to the package Ishkan was to deliver. Maybe wrap one or two bricks, but wrap them so that it will take considerable time to unwrap them. Use many layers of paper, and then plastic. It is supposed to be a priceless object, after all."

Father Ishkan was finally starting to look more relaxed, and the tension showed more on the face of Mark Jamison. Father Mesrop saw his discomfort.

"Mark, you don't belong at this meeting, but if you hadn't shown up when you did and asked the right questions…I shudder to think what would have happened."

"Is there anything I can do to help?" Jamison inquired.

"We can handle this, can't we, Father Ishkan?" He turned back to the monk. "You are closest with the captain of police. Can you explain the sensitive nature of this to him without arousing suspicions?"

Jamison felt compelled to speak up. "Father Mesrop, please assume that all your phones are being monitored. You may want to make calls from an outside line or borrow a mobile phone from someone unconnected with the order."

"Thank you again, Mark. Pray for us tomorrow."

Mark wished them good luck and left with a very uneasy feeling. It was time to catch the 5:00 p.m. vaporeto back to Venice and walk to the hotel. Hopefully Sarah hadn't bought out all the shops.

29

Mark's return by boat and his stroll back to the Tre Rose were troubled. He knew the following day wouldn't go as easily as Father Mesrop had envisioned, but he didn't know what to do about it. To help clear his mind of these troubles for a few minutes, at least, he recalled his memories of an earlier stay at the small hotel, which was then called the Patria Tre Rose, when he and Sarah had included it in their honeymoon travels. Everything seemed so long ago. Tonight he would take Sarah out for a proper dinner to celebrate their return to this magical place and the timeliness of their visits to San Lazaro. He couldn't wait to tell her about the exciting day she'd missed.

He was surprised to not see her waiting for him in their room. He called her cell phone, but another voice answered. "Mark, this is Carol Durlen. We were expecting to hear from you. Malcolm arranged dinner for the four of us this evening, so we picked Sarah up at the hotel and are currently at Harry's Bar."

"Good to speak with you, Carol, but why didn't Sarah answer?'

"She just stepped into the ladies room, and we didn't want to miss your call, so she left her phone with us. Here, let me have you speak with our host for this evening."

Malcolm Wyle's voice rang out from Sarah's cell phone. "So, how soon can you join us? We're having cocktails with your lovely wife and enjoying hearing all about you and the family. Sarah just went to freshen up. Don't worry about finding us. You can't miss us."

"Well, this is really a surprise, Malcolm. How did you manage to find us?"

"Actually, it was a fluke—more than a fluke, really. Carol and I were at a sidewalk café on the square when Sarah walked right past us. I called out to her, and we agreed to get together this evening."

"Funny…She didn't call to tell me about it."

"Well, she said you were involved in a special project at San Lazaro and didn't want to disturb you."

"I see. Well, could you have her phone me when she returns to the table?"

"Certainly. I'm sure it won't be long."

Mark's stomach twisted into a knot. They had Sarah, and if he joined them, they could keep both of them, but they might let her go. If he didn't go, they might figure out he was on to them, and then she would be in real trouble. His mind spun through all the options he could muster.

When the phone rang, it was Sarah, but she sure didn't sound like her usual self. "Please join us as soon as you can, sweetheart." She never called him "sweetheart," and he didn't think she would choose this moment to begin unless there was trouble.

"Is anyone else with you, Sarah?"

"No, just the three of us until you get here."

"Give me twenty minutes. I love you." He hoped she'd pick up on his awareness of the situation. She knew the last part signaled his awareness that she was feeling very vulnerable.

When Mark arrived, the group had moved into the dining room. He scanned his eyes across Harry's Bar, looking for anyone else whom he might recognize, but saw no one. He briefly thought of calling the police, but he had no solid knowledge that a crime had been committed. Besides, they would only make a mess of it. He thought that a gun in a shoulder vest would feel reassuring, but he had nothing, so he summoned his diplomatic smile and pushed ahead into the dining room.

"Malcolm and Carol! What an amazing coincidence." He leaned over to kiss both Sarah and Carol and then shook Malcolm's hand, saying how thoughtful it was of Wyle to host him and Sarah, before he sat down.

"So, what brings you both to Venice?" Jamison took the initiative in the conversation.

Carol responded that after Urumqi and Moscow, she'd needed some time to unwind, and Malcolm had some legal work in the area. "He's so thoughtful, really," she said, looking at Wyle with a disingenuous smile. "And you, Mark? Sarah says you have been digging into the past out at San Lazaro."

"Futilely, as it turns out, but I had to follow up on earlier visits to Jerusalem and Armenia. I guess what's buried in the past will stay buried. We'll be heading out tomorrow."

"That's sudden, isn't it?" Sarah asked. "I was hoping for more adventure on this trip."

Mark winced internally and responded. "I was thinking that we could rent a car and drive across northern Italy for a few days before heading back to California, maybe go back to Sirmione at Lago di Garda." He turned to Carol and Malcolm and relayed that on their last visit, the fog was so thick that they couldn't even find the lake. He knew that both Malcolm and Carol were trying to figure out if he knew what they had planned for tomorrow.

"Have you all ordered? I understand the *Carpaccio* is a specialty," Mark remarked as casually as he could.

"Let's get you a drink first, Mark," Malcolm said as he waved a finger for the waiter. "What will you have?"

Mark spoke directly to the waiter. "A Montgomery martini with Belvedere vodka and two olives, please."

"Anyone else?" Malcolm asked. "Of course, we'll be having Italian wines with dinner."

"I look forward to your selections." Mark smiled as sincerely as he could at Wyle, who winked in response.

"Okay, I can't resist. Mark, what's a Montgomery martini?" asked Wyle.

"Something with practically no vermouth that was named after the field marshal—Hemingway is reputed to have enjoyed them. They're served without a stemmed glass." Mark tried to relax as much as possible, and then Carol spoke up.

"You know, Mark, before you arrived, Sarah and I were discussing going up together tomorrow and having a look around the area from the air. She knows about my flying you around, and now she's game to give it a go. You boys can come too if you'd like, of course. I rented a small four-seater—a seaplane, with pontoons. Could be a lot of fun!"

Mark felt like he'd been squeezed into a very tight space without air.

Sarah spoke up. "Sweetheart, we could leave on our trip the following day. It would be great to see the place by air, and I've never been on an airplane that landed or took off from the water before."

"Neither have I, Sarah, but I really think we should be moving on." Mark knew he was threading through a minefield.

"I may go along too, Mark—should be spectacular—but I need to check with the office in the morning to be sure," Wyle added most unhelpfully.

Then came the bombshell that Jamison had wanted so much to avoid. Sarah asked him, "So, how did the follow-up meeting with Father Ishkan go today?" Mark nearly fell out of his chair and through the floor.

"He didn't have anything. He knows a little about Byzantine chess, but that's about all." Mark knew Carol Durlen was staring at him, and he couldn't bring himself to look back at her. He knew he couldn't lie that well, try as he might. He just knew that she knew he was lying. His pulse started to race.

Wyle casually commented, "You know, we visited San Lazaro ourselves recently, and Carol foolishly left her laptop there. When we phoned over, your good Father Ishkan promised to deliver it to us tomorrow. I'm going to give him a generous reward for it, but only after we look it over and make sure it's the real thing—there are a lot of counterfeits floating around here. I will have to make sure before he gets his reward."

The statements were now thinly veiled. With them, Mark realized that Father Mesrop's plan for tomorrow would quickly unravel. These were no fools. They would not part with $20 million for a few well-wrapped masonry bricks. *When that deception is revealed*, Mark realized, *these folks are liable to do anything. Now they are trying to get Sarah into the middle of it all.* Mark wanted to swallow hard, but couldn't find enough moisture in his throat to do it.

The conversation proceeded in fits and starts for the rest of the evening. Carol was succeeding at building a friendship with Sarah even as he couldn't bring himself to look Carol in the eye. He got through the dinner by talking with Wyle about his precious oil deals and his manipulative transactions with Domich. Mark even pretended to still be interested in the firm, even though they both knew that Victor, with his sore shoulder, would as soon throw him under a bus as hire him.

As he looked at Wyle and pretended to listen to him, Mark imagined him saying, *This man Ishkan will have to show us what he has. I'll have my expert along to make sure everything is real. If the deal goes wrong, your wife will ride away with us until we level off at 20,000 feet, and then we'll push her out the door.* Jamison could envision their rage at finding bricks and could hear Sarah screaming as she was shoved out the door by Gottlieb, who would be lurking in the back of the plane.

Did they really find Sarah at San Marco Square, or did they know where to find her and come after her at the hotel? Mark asked Sarah as casually as he could about where they'd run into each other. Mark cringed when she said they phoned the hotel and asked for her. "I thought you all had arranged it beforehand," she said.

All pretense evaporated. Mark said he wasn't feeling well and wanted to get back to the hotel for an early night. As he stood by Sarah's chair to escort her out, Carol said that she and Malcolm would join them to make sure they got back safely. They took a taxi back. To his surprise and relief, Carol and Malcolm allowed Sarah to leave with Mark. Each party assured the other of an early phone call to confirm who would be joining Carol for the flight.

Mark's head was spinning when they got back to their room. At first he thought it was his troublesome vertigo returning, or maybe just the incredible tension from what had transpired, but then he noticed a strange chemical taste in his mouth and asked Sarah if she'd noticed it, too. Before he could hear her response, he collapsed, unconscious, onto the bed. When he awoke, he found himself still fully dressed. It was light outside, and Sarah was gone.

CHAPTER

30

His forehead ached from what had been slipped into his drink the night before. He stared at the telephone, not knowing what to do. Sarah's purse and cell phone were on the floor. He called the front desk to see if they might have seen or heard something last night or early this morning, but they hadn't. He asked if there had been any messages or visitors asking about them in the lobby, but there were none. He told them that his wife was missing and to keep their eyes open for any sign of her. When they asked if he wanted the hotel to call the police, he said not just yet. Before hanging up, he asked that a pot of hot coffee be sent up to his room.

His mind raced. The phone rang—it was the front desk.

"Mr. Jamison, there was a message for you in the very early morning, but the night clerk seems to have misplaced it. We are very sorry. We are trying to contact her now and will let you know what we find out."

This was not at all what he needed to hear. The coffee arrived a few moments later, and the fog covering the chemical taste lifted enough to confirm that something close to poison was used to put him out. The night clerk must have seen someone enter and given them the room key, unless the clerk was lying unconscious somewhere.

The phone rang again, and he grabbed it off the hook, hoping for some word about Sarah. There was silence on the other end, then laughter—unmistakable laughter.

"Hello my dear friend!" It was Hani's voice.

"Hani, there is so much going on. Where are you now?"

"Actually, closer than you think."

"When can you get here?"

There was a soft knock on the door. Mark opened it slightly, and there stood his old friend.

"Told you I was near," Hani joked. As they hugged, Mark pulled him into the room.

"Can I pour you a coffee? Sit down. When did you get in?"

"Early flight landed at 9:10. Came straight here. Yes for coffee, please."

"Hani, I didn't know what to do until this minute. Sarah is missing. It's a long story that I'll share with you on the way to San Lazaro, but I'm certain she's been kidnapped. You okay to walk with me to catch the vaporeto?"

"Anywhere you say. …So it *is* San Lazaro. I knew it!"

As they headed out past the lobby, Mark stopped, wrote out a message, and sealed it in an envelope before handing it to the clerk on duty. "Here, give this to the police if I am not back here by seven o'clock. If my wife shows up, call me immediately at this number, and don't let her leave the hotel again with anyone until I arrive. Understood?"

"Yes, sir."

Mark turned to Hani. "Let's get out of here, but before I tell you what's going on, you have to tell me who told you to come to Venice immediately."

"It was the Russians. You know I work for everyone. One of my Russian contacts phoned me and said it was urgent. I was doing some work with the Palestinians—they'll have to wait a little longer."

The two were walking quickly, and they would take a water taxi the moment they arrived dockside. "So, Hani, had any more to do with Malcolm Wyle recently?"

"What, you mean the ambassador?"

"He hasn't been that in a long while. He works with Domich&Carey now."

"The law firm? Yes, it is certainly well known...So he's there now. That makes sense. They are global powerbrokers."

"Ever work for them or see Wyle again after our time together?"

"Look, Mark, I work to resolve disputes. Those folks cook them up."

"So the answer is no? Hani, I'm deadly serious about this. Wyle made it seem that he was staying in touch with you, or at least knew how to reach you."

"Never saw him again after our time together in Oman. That was a long time ago, Mark."

Mark stopped to look into Hani's eyes, and Hani saw that tears were forming in Mark's eyes.

"Mark, whatever it is, I am here for you. You know that."

Mark nodded in acknowledgement, and they continued at a fast pace to the dock and boarded a water taxi. "When we get to the island, I will introduce you to its director, Father Mesrop. Our goal is to have you spend some time there with Father Ishkan, San Lazaro's chess master. He knows a great deal about Byzantine chess, and I want you to find out how much. He has documents from the Persians about the game going back to around 600 AD."

"Mark, this is fantastic news, but the documents would be in ancient Persian."

"I am told that he has been working on a book about what he has uncovered over his years on the island, and the linguists on San Lazaro can tackle any language from that part of the world, even the ancient languages. I would bet his book, or at least his manuscript, is in English, Italian, or modern Armenian. In any event, that would be easy to read or have translated...Did you know that Lord Byron lived with these monks? He even wrote books in Armenian."

"I understand. This will be quite a day for me, to be sure, but tell me about Sarah. What in the world has happened to her?"

"Hani, you'll know everything about that tonight. For now, I want you to focus on Father Ishkan and learning all you can from him. If there are secret plays or strategies to be learned, there is a huge need for them now, to help bring an end to the chaos of this world. I am turning him over to you knowing that you will do the right thing with whatever you learn. I know he wants the same thing we want."

As the boat docked, Mark led Hani Waladoon to Father Mesrop's office and presented him and a summary of his credentials. "Then you *are* the Game Master," Father Mesrop marveled. "My good fellow, you really belong here with us. We are at your disposal."

"Father, I would like Hani to spend the day with Father Ishkan and to learn all that he can from him. I assure you that whatever he learns will be used only to help mankind," Mark assured the monk.

"With these assurances and the guarantee of the physical safeguard of everything on this island, I give you both my blessings and my full cooperation. Deacon David will be here in a few moments to escort Mr. Waladoon. Mark, I hope you might remain with me to continue our discussion from yesterday."

"I was hoping the same thing, Father."

As Hani departed with Deacon David, Father Mesrop invited Mark to sit down.

"Father Ishkan decided not to contact the police this morning and wants to conclude this matter without public embarrassment of himself or the order, and I am sure he is also interested in protecting his brother and the rest of his family. I couldn't argue with him—if the police get involved, there is no telling where an investigation may lead. I will allow no investigations on this island. We have always been treated like our own sovereign state here, and I will not jeopardize this. Nothing will leave this island but an old briefcase and a few bricks, so I am not so worried about involving the police."

"Father, there is a new complication that I want to discuss with you. I think it will make this plan more challenging."

As Mark explained his knowledge of the British woman and the American gentleman who had been in contact with Father Ishkan, Father Mesrop sat transfixed. When Mark accounted for the events of the last night and the disappearance of Sarah, Father Mesrop's face fell into his hands. Both sat silently while each fully absorbed the gravity of the situation.

"We must protect Sarah at all costs," Father Mesrop pronounced, "even if it means bringing in the police. What are your thoughts, Mark?"

"Let me ask you two questions. First, can you get hold of a fast boat by this afternoon and find someone here to drive it?"

"Well, I can certainly arrange the boat with the casino on the Lido—they have a speed boat that I'm sure they will lend me—and Deacon David loves fast boats. He told me that he used to race them on the Charles River near MIT."

"Excuse me, Father, but did you say you could get a boat from the *gambling* casino on the Lido? I didn't suspect you would even know those people."

"Mark, we are a religious order that enjoys an occasional wager with God's blessing and assistance, and some of the order do pretty well. We have a fine reputation, and the manager says we are good for business whenever we are around. What is the second question?"

"Do you think you could find a rifle and some ammunition?"

"Yes, I could find several rifles, but I caution you that none of the order shoots straight."

"That's perfect, Father Mesrop. Let me share what I have in mind and see what you think."

The two discussed Mark's plan for the next hour and then took their lunch together in the dining hall. They both nodded approvingly as they saw Father Ishkan and Hani Waladoon in rapt conversation there.

Later in the afternoon, Mark met with Hani and Father Ishkan to see how they were progressing. "Mark, it's fantastic beyond words. Father Ishkan has tied the pieces together. He is a brilliant man!" Father Ishkan beamed at Hani's compliment.

"Well, we have a dress rehearsal in the auditorium at four o'clock with Father Mesrop, so I'll see you both there."

"Dress rehearsal for what?" Hani asked Father Ishkan.

"For my redemption, Hani. Come and find out."

The afternoon passed quickly in a flurry of activity among the monks. Soon it was 5:45 p.m., and the monastic order's old launch prepared to get under way with Father Ishkan and the briefcase. Mark Jamison was by his side. They went to the appointed area for the rendezvous and cut the engine.

Soon a single-engine seaplane appeared in the sky, circled once, and landed nearby. Father Ishkan started the engine and proceeded to the floating aircraft as arranged. The cabin door opened and Carol Durlen called out, "He'd better have it with him! And what are you doing here, Mark?"

"Carol, I came to ask you to reconsider this. No one has called the police, so you are free to call this off with no harm done. Is Sarah on the plane?"

"Hello Mark," Malcolm called out as he maneuvered to present Sarah at the doorway. Her mouth was gagged and her arms were bound together.

"You folks seem to have a habit of getting my family all tied up. Release her now, and no one will be the wiser," Mark implored. "Gottlieb with you, too?"

"Of course. Someone needs to make sure you're not substituting something else for what we bargained for."

"Release Sarah, and you'll get away clean. No one will report anything."

"We'll leave with what we came here for."

"Then release Sarah, and you'll get what you bargained for," Mark promised as he pointed to Father Ishkan, sitting wide-eyed in his black habit with the briefcase on his lap. "You can withhold your briefcase of money until you verify the goods, but you have to release Sarah first."

"Sarah stays here, and so does our exchange. Now give us the briefcase or we'll be prying it from dead fingers."

Father Ishkan stood up, and the signal was delivered. Shots rang out from a speedboat that was fast approaching and carrying seven rifle-bearing monks, their black habits flaring in the wind.

"Give it to me now," Malcolm ordered as he stretched to receive the briefcase. More shots rang out, and Father Ishkan suddenly grabbed his chest and fell forward into the water, still holding the briefcase. As Malcolm jumped on the plane's pontoon and bent down, Mark yanked him into the water. With his left arm, he reached up and grabbed Carol's arm, tossing her over the side as well.

"Come on Sarah, get out of there," Mark shouted as he kept Carol and Malcolm from climbing into his boat. When Wyle persisted, Mark reached back into the boat and grabbed an oar, which he swung directly into Wyle's head. Wyle slumped down in the water.

"Better rescue your partner, Carol," Jamison commanded as he pulled the unharmed Father Ishkan back into the boat, the worthless briefcase rapidly descending into the depths of the lagoon.

"Come on, Sarah," he implored as she stood frozen. He noticed a small pistol that Gottlieb aimed at her.

"It's over, Gottlieb. You have a choice, here: If you really have $20 million in there, hand it over and toss your gun overboard. I'll testify that there were two hostages on the plane. If you don't, I'm going to tell this rapidly approaching boatload of armed Armenian clergy that a

Turkish spy is holding my wife at gunpoint. They have long memories around here."

Jamison watched Gottlieb jump into the water and assume the pose of rescuer as the boat of Armenian clergy, bearing the logo *Casino de Veneto* pulled alongside. From the opposite direction, an Italian customs boat was coming on very fast. Malcolm and Carol were hanging silently onto the gunnels of the monastic order's boat, with Sarah and Gottlieb now safely aboard. F.C. Gottlieb gently took off Sarah's gag and bindings and tossed them into the sea.

"So, Franz, where's the $20 million?" Mark asked jocularly as he looked as Father Ishkan.

Gottlieb pulled out a soggy envelope with a bundle of Euros amounting to about $120,000. He held out the money, and the Italian customs authorities grabbed the envelope and put handcuffs on Gottlieb. If he could provide the documentation for the funds, Mark knew, he would be released. Otherwise, the importation to Italy of that amount was a felony.

"Who are the people in the water, and why is that man's head bleeding?" a customs official asked.

"They were trying to sell the airplane to this gentleman with the money, but weren't able to show proof that they owned it. I think that's called wrongful appropriation and fraud, which are also felonies here in Italy," Jamison said, enjoying the moment. The customs people pulled Ms. Durlen and Mr. Wyle out of the lagoon and asked if that was true, but neither said anything. Handcuffs went on both, and they were escorted onto the customs boat to join Gottlieb.

"Now, why are all those Armenian monks on the casino boat?" the customs officer asked.

"My understanding is that they got special permission from the head of their order for an evening of gambling at the Lido, and the casino provided the boat. They were on their way when they saw their own boat out here trying to rescue the owners of the plane. I was visiting the island and asked to come along. Apparently, the purchaser became very unhappy when they couldn't show title to the airplane and threw them both overboard. Can the monks be allowed to proceed along to the casino?"

"One more question, first: There were reports of gunfire from this area."

"This old boat's engine backfired very loudly getting here. Father Ishkan was about to take it for servicing when we saw the trouble here."

"That's enough for my report. You may all leave now."

Mark looked at Sarah. "Want to go gambling with the monks? You asked for an adventure today, and almost got one."

CHAPTER

31

The Vatican—Present Day

Popov and Jamison arrived at the Mater Ecclesiae surprised to find Hani Waladoon playing Byzantine chess with retired Pope Benedict, who appeared to be winning the game. They stood, watching from the doorway, as the former pontiff said, "You see, dear Hani, the moves work better than anyone could have imagined."

"Wait a minute," Jamison called out, entering the study. "You mean you actually defeated Hani? You had the moves all along?"

"I only got them after the final game to resolve the location in which the seat of the Third Rome would be established," the former Pontiff replied. "Come in and sit down. It's good to see you both."

Jamison looked quizzically at Hani only to hear his unmistakable laughter.

"So, what is going on here, gentlemen?"

The retired pontiff looked at Hani before responding for both of them.

"It's all done, you see. Popov, you'll be learning this soon enough—better to hear it from me."

"The Russians played for Moscow, of course," the Pontiff explained, "but in the end, we prevailed. It was best out of three. The Third Rome has come home to the seat of the first Rome.

"Francis and I are delighted, of course, because neither of us wanted to move. Our Italian is as good as our Spanish and German—well, nearly so—and neither of us would be able to stand the winters in Russia, though global warming is helping a bit, I am told."

"You mean it's already decided, then?"

"It is."

"How will the unification proceed?"

"I think you will like this, Mark. Pope Francis suggested a new Christian ecumenical council to follow that of Nicea and Edessa. There was agreement with this idea, so long as it would be called the Council of Echmiadzin. No one could think of a more suitable location than the halls there, which are adjacent to the world's oldest Christian cathedral.

"Even though the new unified Church will have its center here in Rome, there was much give and take with the Orthodox Church about the partisan legacy of the title of Pope, and Francis has agreed to take the new title of Catholicos of all Christians."

Mark and Popov were thunderstruck. Popov said, "Your Holiness, my president agreed to all this?"

"Popov, he positively insisted upon it. We finally have a harmony that is truly inspiring. Do you know what else your president announced after the games and follow-up meetings?"

"Please tell me."

"He told everyone that he would be the first to be rebaptized in the new unified Christian church and will be coming to Rome for this purpose in three weeks' time, allowing some room for us to work out the details of the new baptism sacrament with the Latin and Orthodox rites."

Silence fell and lingered. Hani rose up to hug his old friend, and the two kissed each other on both cheeks.

Jamison looked at Pope Benedict and to Popov. "You see, Holy Father? The prophecies were entirely correct. You were the penultimate Pope."

"Yes, yes, and without the need of an Armageddon—there is truly a divine Father who watches over us, and his Messengers were as correct as every prophecy told."

"How about you, Constantine?" Mark asked. "Is this enough to convert an old atheist like you?"

"I may be the next in line behind my president."

"And you would be so welcome, my son—so very welcome."

CHAPTER

32

"Well, Holy Father, were you able to bring any resolution to the Great Game?" Jamison felt presumptuous even asking the question after such monumental accomplishments in relation to the Church. There was silence as Benedict looked at Hani, who looked back at him for a few moments and then burst out laughing.

"Ah, yes, the Great Game. The outcome was never in doubt, was it Hani?"

"There was a week of preliminary meetings followed by two days of games devoted to this," Benedict explained. "Everyone was in earnest owing to the circumstances—the missing aircraft threatened an Electro Magnetic Pulse over the USA, Europe, and Russia, and even over China and India. This would be the end of all that these nations had achieved and were still working to achieve. There needed to be unity of purpose, a unity of resolve, and an end to the nonsense, and everyone who attended knew this very well. There was agreement as to most areas, using game resolution to bring about final decisions. The diplomatically irresolvable issues were put to final up-or-down-resolution through the games."

"Judging by Hani's laughter, the outcome couldn't have been too dire?"

"Remember, dear Mark and Constantine, that the greatest danger is from indecision, which is the worst sort of decision making. The negotiations went well enough, and the final decisions through the games were successful. All Hani did was play to win. What was wagered by the parties on the outcome of the games was unknown to the players, including Hani. At the conclusion, he was briefed on the main points—in total confidence, of course, just like everything we have shared for so long," Benedict said, looking at Jamison and Popov.

"In the end, the history books may fairly conclude that the Great Game was resolved by a game, or a series of games, to be more precise—three out of five, though I do hope the books will omit that part."

"Mr. Popov," Benedict continued, "you should be very pleased to know that Russia will become the newest member of the European Union and will immediately commence talks for full NATO membership. India and Germany will join China, Russia, the United States, France, and the United Kingdom as permanent members of the United Nations Security Council. Oh, and the single-nation veto within the Security Council will be abolished."

Hani finally took the floor. "The decisions were reached by participants at the talks and by the urgency of the situation confronted, of course, but there were other forces at work that you must never forget. It wasn't my skills that prevailed—Pope Benedict just beat me in Byzantine chess, and you were both witnesses. What prevailed was the past saving us and allowing us to have a future.

"It was in a real sense the wisdom of those who came many centuries before us that allowed this all to happen. The key they protected for so long was only to be used to save their civilization from utter destruction, and their civilization turned out not to be the Armenians or the Byzantines, but that of all mankind…At least, I'd like to hope that was the case.

"In any event, the knowledge will no longer be available for the unique advantage of any party, because it will soon be well-known across the globe. The Armenians held the treasure for so very long and paid such an incredible price to hold it. Holy Father, I suggest you now use the moves you have learned to teach Monsignor Eke and Archbishop Scheuer the lesson that their old professor still holds a trick or two up his vestment sleeves."

With that, everyone turned to the screeches coming from the suspended cage of Paparrazi, perched above the rubber plant.

"Paparazzi, quiet down," Benedict called out. "You're molting again in all this excitement.

May I offer any of you any of these marzipan delicacies? They're from a bakery near the Spanish steps, but don't let anyone know. It's one of the secrets we still have left."

THE END

CPSIA information can be obtained at www.ICGtesting.com
Printed in the USA
LVOW11s2351190215

427606LV00001B/12/P